This novel is dedicated to all the loyal Flash Gordon fans over the years, and to s-f fans like myself who have wanted to escape the bounds of Earth.

Flash Gordon Book One: MASSACRE IN THE
22nd CENTURY

Flash Gordon Book Two: WAR OF THE
CITADELS

FLASH GORDON BOOK TWO:
WAR OF THE CITADELS

**tempo
books**
GROSSET & DUNLAP
A Filmways Company
Publishers • New York

Flash Gordon Book Two: War of the Citadels
Flash Gordon Copyright © 1980 King Features Syndicate, Inc.
Text Copyright © 1980 Grosset & Dunlap, Inc.
All Rights Reserved
ISBN: 0-448-17215-1
A Tempo Books Original
Tempo Books is registered in the U.S. Patent Office
Published simultaneously in Canada
Printed in the United States

PROLOGUE

It was dark, the stars overhead obscured by a heavy overcast. The chill wind blew tiny, stinging flakes of snow against Flash Gordon's cheeks as he crouched behind a large rock waiting for the machine that had been stalking him for the past two hours.

He had scrambled up the hill to hide in the rocks in sheer desperation just a few minutes ago, flinging himself down on the frozen ground almost completely winded, but with every sense alert for his pursuer. He figured he had put at least a kilometer between himself and the machine over the last forty-five minutes or so, but he knew well that such a scant lead would not allow him much breathing room.

He had taken the only option open to him—had rushed up the hill and had prepared himself for a last-ditch stand on high ground, from an area where he could scan the horizon for the entire 360 degrees.

Standing in a half-crouch he holstered his weapon, lifted a compact set of light-intensifying binoculars to his eyes, and began searching the rock-strewn plain below him in all directions. Then he saw it. No more than a half-kilometer away, to the west. It was the machine, his pursuer, climbing inexorably and unerringly toward his position.

The machine stopped for a moment, its bulbous head raised, and even at this distance Flash could see the dim night illumination glinting off its multi-faceted red eyes, staring directly his way.

He dropped back down behind the large boulder and took a deep breath of the thin, cold atmosphere, letting it out slowly as he put the binoculars back in their case strapped to his hip. He pulled out his pistol to check the charge.

It was nearly full, but that did not mean very much. As he had learned the hard way on other occasions—the very hard way—the machine coming at him this moment was difficult to put out of commission. Almost impossible, as a matter of fact. There were only a couple of vital areas on the thing's body, which was only slightly smaller than Flash's two-meter, one-hundred-kilo frame. One of them was a small control center on its back, less than a half-centimeter in diameter; the other was a hairline opening at the edge of each eye. Everywhere else, so far as Flash knew, the machine was invulnerable to attack from his pistol, and certainly from any kind of hand-to-hand combat.

He tried to make his brain work, to think his way out of this situation as the android Martin had drilled into his head over and over again during the past two months.

"You must learn to reason like they do if you are to have any chance of success," the droid had said. "You must always remember that your antagonists exist for the sake of battle and for no other purpose. Combat in any form is their prime directive. It is their strength. And if you have the ability to make it so, that prime directive can be their weakness as well."

Two months, Flash thought bitterly, and in all that time he felt he had learned next to nothing. The task ahead of him seemed nearly impossible. Especially so at this moment.

He cautiously raised himself up far enough so that he could see over the rock. The machine was below him now and slightly to the north, but only a couple of hundred meters away. Immediately it stopped and looked directly at Flash, who ducked back behind the rock as a searing pinpoint of light blasted away a huge chunk of the boulder, sending bits of molten rock splattering everywhere.

It was a mistake coming up here. Flash could see that now. The machine below him would not have to move from its spot. It could remain below and slowly but surely blast every boulder off the hillside until Flash had no place else to hide. And from this distance there was no possibility that Flash could hit one of the machine's vital areas with his pistol.

Think! The single word screamed through his brain. And suddenly he had it. Suddenly it was clear to him what he was going to have to do. The machine below him wanted combat. Not merely murder. Combat.

Flash pulled out his pistol and in a crouch darted
away from the large boulder, rolling to the left at
the last moment behind another, much smaller pile
of rocks. The machine below fired another shot,
slightly burning Flash's right leg with a spray of
molten rock.

He cried out in more pain than he felt while he
desperately searched his immediate area for something very specific.

The machine fired again, blasting away one of
the larger rocks nearby as Flash found what he was
looking for. He bobbed up and then immediately
back down, catching just a glimpse of the machine
almost directly below him and less than fifty meters
away. Again the machine fired, dislodging another
rock.

Flash cried out even louder this time and then
threw his pistol over the pile of rocks down at the
machine.

For several long moments there was absolute silence, and Flash strained to hear over the wind if
the machine was stationary or still climbing. Satisfied that the machine was not moving, Flash
cautiously got to his feet and stepped away from
the protection of the rocks.

The machine looked up, its weapon pointed his
way, its huge red eye staring.

It existed for combat. That's what Martin had
said. Combat. Not merely murder.

Flash carefully moved to the base of a large
boulder perched precariously on the hillside and,
from the frozen ground beneath it, pried loose a
fist-size stone, one of several holding the boulder
from rolling downhill. He hefted it a moment in his

right hand, and then threw it with all of his might down at the machine, which casually watched the rock fly, then pointed its weapon up, blowing it out of the sky.

Flash laughed, bent down and pried loose a couple more of the rocks, throwing them one at a time at the machine, which impassively blasted them and then began moving slowly up the slope.

In earnest now, Flash got down on his hands and knees and frantically began digging the rocks and loose dirt from the base of the boulder as the machine came closer and closer up the hill. He had not engaged in hand-to-hand combat with any of the machines so far, and he did not want to begin now, so he redoubled his efforts.

He looked up finally as the machine was less than five meters away, then jumped up and rushed around behind the huge rock and put his shoulder to it. It moved slightly, and Flash shoved harder, setting up a rocking motion.

The machine, apparently realizing what was about to happen, tried to scramble backward while firing at the huge boulder, but suddenly the massive chunk of granite-like material broke loose and began ponderously rolling, slowly at first, down the hill, but gathering momentum rapidly.

At the last moment the machine tried to move sideways out of the boulder's path, but it was too late, and the huge rock slammed into the machine, crushing it amid a shower of sparks and a spurt of its hydrodynamic fluid. It careened over the machine and then past the broken remains, crashing all the way down the hill.

As Flash got to his feet from where he had fallen

when the boulder had given way, the wind died, the snow stopped falling, the temperature began to rise, and the lights in the huge testing center came up.

Flash brushed himself off as he started down the long hill, and in the distance he could see a groundcar approaching across the plain.

For nearly two months he had been going through this sort of thing, with variations, while Dr. Hans Zarkov was learning the planet's computer systems and Dale Arden was working with the crew of the Goodhope on a Citadel defense system.

At the bottom of the hill, Flash waited by the dirt road for the groundcar to reach him, thinking about all that had happened to them over the past fantastic weeks. He tried once again to make some sense out of what they would eventually have to do.

It had begun when the Federation exploration vessel Goodhope had been discovered in deep space and towed back to Earth orbit by a Trans Federation company cargo vessel.

It had been two-and-a-half months ago and 165 light years away from here, when Dr. Zarkov had been called in by the military to attempt to board the Goodhope.

The exploration vessel had been sent into deep space two hundred years earlier, before the time that faster-than-light drive had been invented. When Zarkov, his niece Dale Arden, and Flash had entered the Goodhope they had found all but one of its 158-member crew murdered—their throats slashed. The missing crew member was a young woman named Sandra Debonshire.

Flash shook his head trying to sort out in his memory all the strange things that had happened to them.

Trans Federation, the most powerful—and some said malevolent—multiplanet corporation in the Federation, which had laid salvage claims to the Goodhope, had sent a crew up to burn its way aboard the vessel when it automatically took off, jumped into hyperspace, even though it supposedly didn't have that capability, and finally crash-landed on this planet, which they later learned was called Citadel I. Flash, Dale, and Dr. Zarkov, on board the Goodhope trying to unravel the two-hundred-year-old murder mystery, barely managed to escape on a shuttle vessel that was itself destroyed in a hard landing, stranding them on this planet.

Then, step by inexorable step, they were led to the planet's only city, which had been built more than twenty thousand years earlier by the remnants of a once-powerful galactic civilization that had died away after a colossal war lasting more than eighty thousand years. The enemy was another great and powerful civilization across the galaxy.

The groundcar was less than a kilometer away now as Flash turned and looked back up the hill at the remains of the machine he had fought.

The machine represented the technology of the other civilization. A civilization that had constructed a vast computer in a hollowed-out planet, much like the one Flash was on now, only across the galaxy.

This planet, Citadel I, and the other civilization's

repository of knowledge, called Citadel II, were all
that was left of the two once-mighty civilizations—
one existing for peace, the other for war.

Flash turned as the groundcar pulled up alongside him, and Martin, the caretaker droid of
this Citadel planet, beckoned for him to climb
aboard. The robot seemed worried.

"I stopped it," Flash said, getting into the low
machine. "My method was a little crude, perhaps,
but it worked." He spoke in the language Martin
had taught them all.

Martin looked at Flash. "We have troubles, Col.
Gordon," he said. And Flash was certain he could
detect a genuine note of worry in the android's
voice and features, something he had come to learn
was possible despite the fact that Martin was nothing more than a machine.

Flash, Dale, Dr. Zarkov, and the crew of the
Goodhope, all 158 of whom they had found paradoxically alive and well on this planet, had agreed
to help when they learned that the Citadel II planet
was planning someday to continue the war their
builders had started and then abandoned thousands of years ago.

A hundred and twenty years ago the Goodhope's crew, in deep sleep, had been awakened
by Martin, who had come out to their ship
aboard a faster-than-light drive vessel. He transported the crew back here, and explained the history of the Citadel worlds. He asked them to help
organize the knowledge contained in the computer
so that someday the Federation of Planets, with its
base on Earth, could share the hard-won wisdom
of a fabulous civilization dead and gone now for

twenty thousand years.

The crew, under Capt. Van d'Hoef, had agreed to help, even though they understood it would mean their own deaths, or at least the death of their biological bodies, and that it might be a thousand years or more before mankind as a whole would be ready to handle the vast knowledge.

Because the Goodhope would have been eventually found by the expanding Federation, Sandra Debonshire, the ship's psychologist, had volunteered to return to the Goodhope at faster-than-light speed to a point in time before Martin had arrived to take them to the Citadel. On board she murdered the sleeping crew and threw her own body out an airlock. When the Goodhope was finally found, it would seem as if she had gone insane and had murdered her fellow crew members before committing suicide.

Once back on Citadel, the crews' psyches were imprinted on biological androids, indistinguishable from real human beings, and they had been living and working now on Citadel I for more than 120 Earth years toward the day they could return home with the knowledge of the ancient civilization that built the Citadel.

"It has begun," Martin said softly.

Flash sat forward in his contour seat. "What?" he said.

"It has begun. A scout ship appeared out of hyperspace and is presently in a stable orbit some ten thousand kilometers out. We are being scanned."

"That's impossible," Flash said. "You told me that this planet's systems have all been muted, making us impervious to scanning."

Martin was shaking his head. "Our muting systems are inoperative. We're standing out at this moment like a bright beacon on a dark night."

"Inoperative," Flash said with a chill, "or sabotaged."

CHAPTER 1

Dr. Zarkov was with two of the Goodhope's technicians in the Citadel's operations center two thousand kilometers below the surface of the planet when Flash and the android Martin arrived on one of the transplanet shuttles.

The center was one of eight huge control points for the mammoth, planetwide computer system, entrance to which was gained through a matter transmitter portal on one side of a low, octagonal building in the center of a vast subterranean park.

In their two months here, Zarkov had begun to alter the computer's control-point functions so that a human being with five-digit hands could adequately master various systems. The builders of the gigantic computer, dead and gone now for more than twenty thousand years, had six-digit hands, each finger with so many joints they were almost liquid, making them very dexterous.

Here at the operations center, Zarkov had only

managed to convert a few of the lesser systems and one data terminal to the simpler controls, and in the interim it took a team of two and sometimes three highly coordinated humans to successfully operate the computer.

Zarkov was calling out numbers and controls while the two Goodhope technicians were doing the actual manipulations.

Overhead, above the large central console, a three-dimensional model of the area of space immediately around the Citadel shimmered in the dim light of the control center. As Flash and Martin entered the room, they both could see immediately that something was happening, or about to happen.

A red speck, which represented the scout ship sent from the other Citadel, was parked in a stable orbit some ten thousand kilometers out, directly over the planet's only city. Another speck, this one green, was arching up from the planet's surface, obviously on an intercept course for the scout ship.

Zarkov was working on a computer subsystem from which a rapid display of numbers and diagrams streamed across a small data terminal. From the information he was receiving he was passing on instructions to the two technicians, who were doing their best to keep up with him.

Flash and Martin stood just within the portal and watched the nearly silent drama unfold overhead. There were no sounds of clattering machinery, no sirens, no flashing lights, only Zarkov's even-paced instructions to the technicians.

"How do you know it's a scout ship from the other Citadel?" Flash asked the android, keeping his voice low as he alternated his gaze from Zarkov to the model overhead.

"Our own automatic scanning systems confirmed it," Martin said, matching Flash's soft tone of voice. "The central data bank has a working model of the other's technology as of the day we came here. From it, new developments are extrapolated, and the scout ship matched one of the projections. It was simple, actually."

"How about our scanner muting system? What happened to it?" Flash asked, his concentration still on the overhead display.

Martin looked at him. "I don't know, Col. Gordon. The computer only shows an unknown malfunction. We're working on it at the moment."

Flash turned to him. "Unknown? Isn't that strange?"

"Very," Martin said, and Flash had the distinct impression that the droid was holding something back from him.

He was about to pursue it further when there was a commotion at the control console. He snapped around in time to see Zarkov rushing over to the section of the console that one of the technicians had been operating.

Overhead, the ship sent up to intercept the intruder was glowing a bright, angry red, a huge rosy halo forming around it.

Flash started to move toward the console, but Martin moved faster than any human could ever move, shoving Zarkov and the others away, none too gently. The robot's fingers played at lightning speed over the console controls as he simultaneously studied a number of subsystem data terminals, across which numbers and diagrams flashed with bewildering rapidity.

Above, the intercept ship was glowing white, so brightly now that it hurt the eyes to look directly at it.

Zarkov had turned pale, and the Goodhope technicians had stepped back to where Flash stood. All of them were watching the unfolding drama overhead.

Martin punched one final button, and then he too stepped back from the console and concentrated his attention on the overhead display.

The intercept ship began veering away, slowly at first, but then faster and faster. The further it got from the intruder, the more muted its glow became. But then something happened that for several moments Flash and the others could not quite believe they had really seen.

The intruder ship suddenly flashed from its position to another ahead of the intercept ship, and in the next instant the intercept ship blossomed in a white flash and disappeared. Then the intruder ship itself was gone. Vanished, with no warning from the sensors.

Both Martin and Zarkov moved back to the console and began querying the computer for further data, but after just a few seconds they both came to the realization that it was hopeless for the moment.

Martin turned around to face the others, and he looked ashen. If he had been a human being, Flash would have been certain he was on the verge of a heart attack.

"It's too late," the android said, his voice weak. "It's already too late. They're ahead of us. It is impossible, but it is true."

Flash moved forward. "What do you mean? Explain yourself."

Martin, who had hung his head in an expression of dejection, looked up. "I think we'd better all meet." He turned to Zarkov, who nodded.

"Look, Flash," the aging scientist said, "the computer extrapolated the other's technology at least to the point where it was able to identify the type of scout vessel. It was unmanned, we know that too. But . . ." He turned to look up at the now-dormant display overhead. "But what it just did, unless I'm mistaken, is beyond even the technology of this Citadel."

Martin nodded his head in confirmation. "Dr. Zarkov is correct, unfortunately. We, that is to say, the machine and I have been working with very little progress on the theory for perhaps a thousand years. But without intuitive reasoning, it has been difficult at best."

"The theory of what?" Flash asked, taking another step forward. The Goodhope technicians, he could see, were just as confused as he was. But it was no measure of consolation.

"Matter-energy transference," Martin said matter of factly. He nodded toward Dr. Zarkov. "The good doctor calls it shadow boxing, whatever that means. However, the concept is the same."

"Explain," Flash barked. He did not understand exactly what was going on, but he knew that whatever had happened would have some bearing on their survival.

Martin seemed to sigh, a mechanical impossibility. "The explanation will wait, I believe, until we are all together. This is something quite serious. Quite serious indeed. We all will have to decide on the next step. If there is one."

Flash looked to Zarkov, who nodded sadly. "I'm afraid I have to go along with him, Flash. Let's all meet and we will explain everything. I can only guess at some of the ramifications, but if the sensor data confirm our suspicions, we are in rather serious trouble."

"All right," Flash said after a long, silent moment. He looked at his chronometer, which had been adjusted to local planet time some weeks ago. It showed the time was shortly after ten in the morning. The period of rotation on this planet was something under twenty-two Earth hours standardized, but all of them had adjusted easily to the shorter days and shorter nights. "Can we get everyone back to the operations center by noon?"

Martin nodded. "I've already initiated the call."

Hand-in-hand with the fact that Flash could not get used to the concept that Martin was only a machine, was the fact that the android was in nearly constant communication with the Citadel's main computer bank. At any moment, given the proper stimulus, Martin had available to him all of the capabilities of the main computer circuitry. It was as if he was little more than a mobile computer terminal, with the added ability of being able to think—to a degree—for himself.

In fact it was Martin himself who had explained that to them all, along with his one overriding limitation. "No matter how sophisticated you may believe I am, I still do not have the ability to reason intuitively. I still need the proper input to bring up information from the main computer banks ... analogous to your own memories. Unlike a living, sentient being, I do not have the ability to spontaneously recall information that has no apparent logical use at the moment. That, reduced to its simplest terms, is intuitive reasoning."

Through the remainder of the morning the Goodhope's crew members arrived singly and in small groups at the meeting room, located far above the city. They came from all over the planet, as well as far below its surface in the bowels of the Citadel computer. Martin's summons was unusual enough to create much speculation and, in a few, some degree of panic, and it wasn't until the ship's captain, Peter Van d'Hoef, arrived with Sandra Debonshire and Dale Arden that there was any order in the center.

Martin and Dr. Zarkov had remained in the computer control center promising they would come up at noon. Van d'Hoef, once he had his people calmed down, came across the large room to Flash and pulled him aside.

"What's going on, Gordon?" the man asked. He seemed mad. "We were just finishing up with the deep space scanner when the call came from Martin that he and Dr. Zarkov wanted to see us all." He looked around the room. "Where are they, anyway?"

"Did you shut off the Citadel's muting system?" Flash asked sharply. "Were you working on it this morning?"

Van d'Hoef turned back. "What do you think I am, crazy? Of course I didn't."

"Someone did," Flash said.

"Now listen," Van d'Hoef started to sputter, but Flash held him off.

"I'm not saying it was you, but something or

someone shut off our muting system, just in time
for our visitor."

It took a moment for what Flash had said to sink
in, but when it did, Van d'Hoef paled. "Visitor?"
he squeaked.

Flash nodded. "A scout ship came into orbit
earlier this morning and scanned us from top to
bottom. Our muting system was off, but our own
scanners typed the ship. It was from the other
Citadel."

"Then it's already started," Van d'Hoef said
softly.

"What do you mean by that?" Flash asked.
Martin had said the same thing.

Van d'Hoef moved a step closer and lowered his
voice. "From the beginning, I mean from the time
we got here, Martin has been telling us that a confrontation between the two Citadels has been a for-
gone conclusion since the planets were constructed.
It's only a matter of time until the other Citadel
figures it's stronger. Then the attack will come."

"A single scout ship hardly constitutes an attack," Flash protested. Something was wrong here.
He had felt it with Martin, and now the feeling was
doubly strong with Van d'Hoef.

"What happened to the ship? Did we capture
it?"

Flash shook his head. "Martin and Dr. Zarkov
sent out an intercept ship, but the intruder destroyed our vessel and just disappeared."

"That's what I was afraid of," Van d'Hoef said.
"About fifty years ago they sent a scout ship out
here and we captured it. The computer downstairs
took it apart, but found nothing beyond what it

expected to find. The other Citadel had come up with nothing new. No unexpected technologies. That was a big holiday around here. The scout ship was on display. It was a big deal. This time, nothing. So when you told me that a scout ship had shown up I immediately knew something was going on, because there's been no announcement."

Dale, who had been deep in discussion with Sandra Debonshire, came across the meeting hall and reached up on tiptoes to peck Flash on the cheek. She was tall, on the thin side, and had long, flaming red hair.

"How'd it go in testing this morning?" she asked brightly.

"Just fine, I guess," Flash said.

She looked around the room. "Where's Uncle Hans?"

"He and Martin should be coming up any moment now. Have you heard anything?"

"About what?" she asked.

Over the two-and-a-half months since they had unexpectedly left Earth orbit together, Flash had come to have a deep respect and strong admiration for the young woman. She was in love with him, and she had said as much a few nights after they had crash-landed on this planet. But in the following months he had not allowed himself to feel anything more for her than respect and admiration. He knew it hurt her, but he also knew she was a patient woman. Years earlier Flash had lost his young wife to a group of off-world smugglers who had brutally murdered her as a warning to Flash. Since that time there had been a part of Flash that refused to lay bare his emotions for fear of being hurt again.

It was unfair to Dale, he knew, as well as to himself. But it was going to take time, a lot of time, before he could change.

"The other Citadel sent a scout ship here that got away this morning," he said.

Dale was about to say something, when there was a flurry of excited voices at the other end of the large room. They all turned in time to see Zarkov and Martin coming through the main doors and head to the front of the room.

Flash, Dale, and Van d'Hoef all moved forward where they found seats near the head of the room, and when everyone had quieted down, Martin began. The android seemed deeply worried, as did Zarkov, who sat in a low chair in front of a large window.

"Ladies and gentlemen, I'm afraid I have some rather startling news for you this noon," the android began.

There was a ripple of murmurs across the room, but then everyone settled down again.

"Shortly after nine this morning, a scout ship of the type from Citadel II materialized from hyperspace into a stable orbit some ten thousand kilometers directly over this city."

There was another ripple of low-pitched voices.

"There are a number of significant differences, however, between this intrusion and the one that occurred some fifty years ago. The first is that our intercept vessel was destroyed."

The audience gasped collectively, but Martin continued without pause. Flash was getting the distinct impression that all of this was somehow being staged, but why or for whose benefit was beyond him.

"The second is that our muting system was shut down, so the scout vessel was able to make a complete scan. At first it was believed that there was a muting system malfunction, and later Col. Gordon suggested that someone may have inadvertently shut it off, but Dr. Zarkov and I now believe that neither was the case. Much to our consternation, we discovered that the scout ship, in all likelihood, had the capability of shutting our muting system down itself."

Martin hesitated long enough for that piece of information to sink in before he continued, and once again Flash had the feeling that the android was holding something back, that he was lying.

"Dr. Zarkov and I have for the last two hours been working in Central Control on the problem of the scout ship that destroyed our intercept vessel and then itself disappeared. We believe we have the answer.

"If we are correct, and we believe the available data confirms this, the scout ship that intruded our system had a matter-energy transference capability. A capability very far in advance of anything we have on this Citadel."

"Can you explain exactly what that is, Martin?" Van d'Hoef said from next to Flash.

"By all means," Martin replied. "We must all understand the problem so that we can decide what our next step is to be. Simply put, the scout vessel that intruded our system this morning had the capability of transferring matter into energy."

"A nuclear reaction," one of the female crew members interrupted.

"That is only one slight and very crude example of the principle," Martin said unperturbed. "The scout ship apparently has the ability to transfer matter into energy, and energy into matter at will. It has the ability to transfer its own matter into a discrete bundle of energy, a tremendous amount of energy, and transmit itself in that manner anywhere it may wish to go. At its destination, it transfers its energy back into matter."

"Something must be lost each time," Flash spoke up. "I mean, there must be energy expended into heat or light or some other form that cannot be transferred back to its original matter state."

"Indeed," Dr. Zarkov said, getting to his feet. "Which is what gave us the clue. The mass of the scout ship was a tiny bit smaller after its battle with our intercept. A bit of matter, quite small to be sure, was lost into a permanent energy state. It would be my guess that the scout ship has on board a piece of matter—perhaps as light as a couple of kilograms—for just such a use. It is the ship's fuel, if you'd like to call it that."

There was a silence in the meeting hall for several long seconds until Van d'Hoef spoke up again. "So what does this mean in terms of our survival?" he asked.

"War," Martin said. The single word, spoken softly, was nevertheless like a gunshot in a church.

A number of the Goodhope's crew jumped up in protest, their voices rising in anger. But it was Sandra Debonshire, the one who had done the murders aboard the Goodhope 120 years ago, whose voice rose above the others, gradually quieting them down.

Flash caught Zarkov's eye, and he shook his head slightly. Zarkov nodded his agreement. He was just as surprised by Martin's announcement as the others. There was something drastically wrong here.

None of them wanted war, however—least of all Sandra Debonshire.

"It would be a war that by your own admission, Martin, we could not hope to win," she shouted. "If the scout ship sent to us does indeed have the capabilities you suggest, we have no defense against it at this time. We would end up like our intercept ship."

"Are you suggesting that we remain here until Citadel II comes for us?" Martin said bitterly. "I was not built for that purpose. My prime directive is to defend this planet and its computer. I intend to do just that."

"And what would you have us do, Martin?" the young woman said. "Build ships, cross the galaxy, and attack Citadel II? Attempt to destroy it?"

"If need be, yes," Martin said. "There is so little time. But you would have a very good chance of success. You are sentient beings who would be doing battle with machines much like myself." He turned toward Flash. "Col. Gordon demonstrated those unique skills this morning when he defeated an advanced soldier-android of Citadel II extrapolated design. Col. Gordon did something no machine would have thought of. It worked."

"I have a better idea," the young woman said. "But it will take some planning, and the cooperation of everyone here."

Instantly half the hands in the room were raised.

"What is your plan?" Martin said, looking directly into her eyes.

"I propose mounting an expedition, immediately, for Centrus, the seat of government and technology of the civilization that built this Citadel."

CHAPTER 2

"If there is an answer to our problem, it will be on Centrus," Sandra Debonshire said.

She, Flash, Dale Arden, Dr. Zarkov, Van d'Hoef, and Martin were seated around a low table in a room just off the main meeting hall. Her suggestion to the others a few minutes ago had caused instant pandemonium, and the six of them had been easily able to sneak off and meet quietly.

Martin had been stunned when she had first made the proposal, and now he was no less shocked. "Whatever for?" he said. "The city, even its remains, is probably no longer there."

"I believe it still will be there," she insisted.

Martin was shaking his head, a human gesture he had picked up from the Goodhope's crew. "There was a great war," he said. "You all know that. I explained everything to you. The war lasted eighty thousand years. No system, no planet, was left untouched. My creators fled Centrus at the last moment to come here with their technology, their literature, and their art. They fled Centrus because it was too late for civilization at the center of the galaxy. The forces from the other beings were on their way at the time to destroy the home planet. There could be nothing left now."

The young woman sighed deeply. "Do you know the coordinates of the system in which Centrus was located?"

"It is no use," Martin argued. "At one time the city was the greatest accomplishment of my creators. At one time it was the seat not only of the galactic government that encompassed millions— literally millions of star systems and tens of trillions of sentient beings—it was the seat of all learning and knowledge. But not now. It is too late. Twenty thousand years too late."

Dr. Zarkov leaned forward in his seat. *"Do* you know the location of Centrus?"

Martin turned to gaze into Zarkov's eyes. "Why?" he asked softly.

Zarkov glanced at the young woman, then directed his attention once again to the android. "I think I understand what Miss Debonshire is getting at."

"I wish you would explain it to me, doctor, because I for one do not."

Zarkov smiled, his manner patient, almost as if he were a parent explaining a difficult concept to a young child. "In your telling of the history of the galaxy, you explained to us that when the galactic federation began falling apart because of the war, several hundred thousand scientists, technicians, and others fled Centrus to this planet where they constructed the city, the Citadel computer, and finally yourself."

Martin nodded uncertainly, and Zarkov continued, still with patience.

"They were men and women much as we are—you also told us that."

"I still don't understand. . . ," Martin started to object, but Zarkov held him off, a certain intensity coming to his voice.

"Your creators had held off a hostile civilization for nearly eighty thousand years, and the last of your brilliant minds were fleeing for their lives. Trying to save whatever they could of all that was good from their lives. All the technology and creativity they possibly could carry with them, they instilled into this Citadel world."

Flash suddenly understood what Zarkov was driving at, and he instantly knew that he could be correct. If Centrus still existed, they might have a chance.

"But they were men fleeing for their lives. They did not have time to bring with them everything that was available. My God, Martin, the mass of knowledge available to them had to have been staggering. Beyond even their own comprehension. On my own home planet, no man can be a master of even a small portion of only one science or technology. Here we are talking about a vast civilization that had millions of years longer than ours to develop. The knowledge had to have been vast even by comparison with this Citadel."

"What you are saying, Dr. Zarkov, is that if Centrus still exists, there may be knowledge there that could help us defend ourselves."

Zarkov nodded. "Yes, that is exactly what I am saying."

"But Centrus no longer exists."

"Are you certain of that, Martin? Have you sent scout ships there? Have you sent probes?"

The android shook his head. "Among my prime directives there was one that I did not inform you of. I felt there was no logical need."

"Which is?"

"There can be no contact between this Citadel and whatever remnants of my creator's civilization remain. The directive was solely for the protection of this planet. Had contact been maintained, the other civilization could have followed the shuttle ships, or subspace communications beam, and wiped this planet out. Everything would have been lost."

Flash was stunned. "Then you don't know where Centrus is?"

Martin turned to him. "I'm afraid I do not, Col. Gordon." He shrugged, another human gesture he had picked up. "Oh, I know within a few thousand light years where the home system is located. I know it was at or near the center of our galaxy. But I know nothing more."

Zarkov had turned away and was lost in thought. When he looked up suddenly, he seemed satisfied with himself. "The computer will know. In its astrogation tanks all stellar system references will use the Centrus system as a base. We merely have to work backward."

"No," Martin said flatly. "Some years ago, after the Goodhope's crew began work here, I attempted to gain that information. I could foresee the time when one of your kind would require that knowledge."

"And?" Sandra Debonshire asked, her eyes alight.

Martin turned toward her. "Nothing. The computer knows nothing."

"You are the computer," she snapped, jumping up. "What I mean to say is, you are nothing more than one of many computer terminals. You just happen to be a mobile terminal. No offense meant," she added.

"My knowledge is the computer's knowledge," Martin objected, but the young woman had already turned her attention away from him.

"Dr. Zarkov, you know more about the computer than anyone else. In two months you figured out more of its systems than all of us put together did in 120 years."

"I had a two-hundred-year head start in the subject," he said.

"Could you find the information?"

Zarkov slowly nodded his head. "I believe so," he said. And he looked up. "If it is there. Martin may be correct, however. Perhaps the Citadel's builders did not include that information in its memory."

"I can't believe that," Sandra Debonshire said. "I will not believe it."

"I cannot help you, and yet I must," Martin said in a strangely strangled voice. There was an obvious struggle building up inside him.

Dale sat forward. "Are your prime directives weighed?" she asked. On Earth Dale's specialty had been computer psychology.

Martin turned slowly toward her. "Yes," he said
with even more difficulty. "But two of them carry
equal weight in my circuitry. One is that I must
resist any and all attempts by Citadel II to destroy
this planet. And the other is that no contact shall
be made between this planet and Centrus or anything that remains of my creators' civilization." He
turned to gaze at Zarkov. "You have created a par-
adox within me. My prime directives, it would
seem, are in this instant mutually exclusive."

"They don't have to be," Dale shot back.

With increasingly erratic movements, Martin
jerked her way.

"You must defend against Citadel II," she said.

The android nodded.

"In order to do that we must discover Centrus."

Martin nodded again, his eyes shining deeply.

"But your prime directive will not allow this
planet—*this* planet, Martin—to have contact with
your creators' civilization, or its remnants."

Martin did not move.

"*We* are not of this planet," Dale said trium-
phantly. "We are of Earth. Without your help we
will find Centrus. Your prime directives will be satisfied."

Martin got unsteadily to his feet. "A fine distinc-
tion, Miss Arden, that is not entirely wasted on me.
But you must understand that my syllogistic
circuitry is somewhat more sophisticated than that.
Acceptance of your logical train of reasoning will
not come easily, if at all."

He looked up as if someone or something in the
distance was calling to him, and when he returned
his gaze to Dale, he seemed even more troubled.

"Miss Debonshire was correct when she termed my function nothing more than a mobile terminal. Much of my circuitry has already been destroyed. Before it is too late, before my function here is totally compromised, I will remove myself from any on-line interface."

"Is that possible?" Zarkov said, getting to his feet.

Martin managed a slight nod. "Yes . . . it can be done . . . there is a place here within the planet that I can go for a time. She . . . the computer will search for me and find me . . . but there may be time for your work . . . time for . . . work."

"How will we find you when we need you?" Zarkov asked.

Martin's head jerked several times, and then his gaze steadied again. "She will find me, especially when it becomes evident what you are doing."

"Isn't our conversation now being monitored? Aren't your circuits automatically relaying our intent?"

Martin shook his head and turned jerkily toward the door. "I have blocked it out temporarily. It is the root of my present difficulty. I must remove my personal memory from her control. Please . . . excuse . . ." The android emitted a strangled gasp, and then rushed out the door and was gone. Van d'Hoef jumped to his feet and started around the table after the machine, but Flash stopped him.

"Leave him!"

Van d'Hoef looked up into Flash's eyes. "I can't," he said. He too seemed to be under a great strain. "He's been . . . like a . . . father to us all. He needs help."

"Yes," Flash said. "And we can best give it to him, and all of us, by doing what has to be done to defend ourselves. We must find Centrus."

"But the prime directive . . . ," Van d'Hoef cried.

"Would be meaningless without the existence of this planet," Flash shouted him down. "Which may well happen unless we can do something about it."

Flash turned to Zarkov. "Can you locate Centrus?" he asked.

"I hope so, Flash," the aging scientist said. "I hope so."

"We'd better not tell the others," Sandra Debonshire said. "Like Peter here, their minds also have been imprinted with the prime directives. We might not be able to handle resistance from them all. I had hoped that Martin would be able to help."

"What about you?" Dale asked. During the two months that she, Flash, and Zarkov had been here, Dale and the young woman had become close friends.

"I'm a murderer, remember, Dale? The act unbalanced me. It was a calculated risk the machine took. It figured I was controllable by the others."

"How about us?" Dale asked. "Haven't we been a threat?"

Sandra looked at her and nodded her head. "It is one of the reasons Martin has been acting so strangely lately." She took Dale's hands. "When you crash-landed, we watched you come in. We knew it was the Goodhope. We knew you were on board, from our scanners. We . . . that is . . . I wanted to go out and pull you off ship. Martin and the others would not allow it. Nor would they allow any search and rescue parties. When you three showed up and then got into the machine's memory, it created quite a stir that still has not been resolved."

"You all have machine memories," Flash said, the sudden revelation coming to him. It explained the odd behavior he had noticed off and on during the two months they had been here.

Sandra Debonshire turned to him. "Not quite, Col. Gordon. We do have our own memories. The computer was very careful with that when we were given our new bodies. I know, because we tested each other on it. Memory-response games and all that. But we are under a certain amount of machine control. That is, the others are. The control of me is imperfect because of what I had to do. The others aren't really aware of how incomplete that control is."

They all automatically turned to Van d'Hoef, who seemed on the verge of hysteria. His mouth was screwed up in a grimace, his eyes were wide, and his nostrils flared.

"No!" he screamed, and he broke away from Flash and rushed for the door.

"Stop him!" the young woman shouted.

Flash raced after the man, catching him just before he hit the door control, spun him around, and clipped him on the jaw with a very controlled right hook. Van d'Hoef went down like a felled ox, Flash catching him in his arms before the man's body could hit the floor.

"What now?" he said looking around. He felt guilty that he had hit the man.

Sandra Debonshire had come around the table, and she helped Flash lay Van d'Hoef's unconscious form down on the floor. "It was the only thing you could have done," she said, as she gently caressed the fallen man's cheek with the back of her right hand.

A moment later she looked around at Zarkov. "How long is it going to take you to search the computer's memory for the Centrus system coordinates?" she asked.

The old man shook his head. "An hour. A day. A week. A year. I don't know. Maybe never."

The young woman seemed to draw inward for a moment, and she glanced again at Van d'Hoef. "Twenty-four hours," she said turning back. "Wherever Martin has gone, I don't think he'll be able to hide his memory for more than twenty-four hours. After that we won't be able to get out of here."

"How about the others?" Flash asked.

"We'll have to leave the back way," Sandra said. "And we're going to have to take Peter with us. If he tells the others what we're trying to do, they'll inform the main data bank."

"How will we get out of here if I do locate the Centrus coordinates?" Zarkov asked. He was obviously deeply troubled.

"In Defense Research, just outside the city, are the latest scout ships. They are constantly being updated by maintenance droids to keep up with the Citadel's research. With Col. Gordon's help, I think I can modify one for our use."

"I'll need Dale's help with the computer," Zarkov said. "I have a data terminal modified for our use in central data control."

Sandra Debonshire got to her feet. "We don't have much time," she said.

"What makes you think we'll find anything of use on Centrus . . . even if it still does exist?" Flash asked.

For a moment the young woman seemed to ponder her answer. "I am an xenopsychologist," she said. "That is, I started out from Earth two hundred years ago as a twenty-two-year-old woman who had been taught what little there was to know about the psychology of nonhuman beings. In the 120 years I've been here I've made my specialty the psychology of the civilization that built this Citadel as well as the other civilization, so far as the computer will cooperate with my research. Centrus still exists—I'm convinced of it. Just as I am convinced that the creators of this Citadel could not have possibly brought with them all the technology available at the time. Our answer is there if anywhere," she said.

"How will we rendezvous when I've finished my search?" Zarkov asked.

Van d'Hoef was beginning to come around, and Sandra Debonshire motioned for Flash to pick him up. They all followed her to the back of the room.

"Listen closely," she said. "On the central data console you'll find a control system for the matter transmitter portal. You'll have to query the computer for it. With the control you will be able to shut off the portal, and when it is time for you to leave, you will be able to transmit yourself anywhere on or in this planet. Twenty hours from now, transmit yourselves to the main seacoast highway outside the city. Flash and I will pick you up there."

"And if we haven't found the Centrus coordinates?" Zarkov asked.

"You must," the young woman said. "Without Centrus everything will be lost." She hesitated a moment. "And that, my fellow humans, includes Earth, and your own Federation, because if Citadel II successfully destroys this planet, the entire galaxy will be theirs for the taking. That would mean domination forever by machines."

"Twenty hours," Zarkov said grimly.

Dale looked into Flash's eyes and was about to say something, but then evidently changed her mind and shook her head. "Good luck, you two," she said, and Sandra Debonshire hit a control that opened a door leading out into the corridor. Around the corner, in the main meeting hall, the crew of the Goodhope was still deep in discussion.

CHAPTER 3

The city was built on the seacoast, within a huge cove. To the south were the flatlands that led, Sandra Debonshire told Flash, eventually to a vast sand desert. To the north were the jungle-covered foothills where Flash, Zarkov, and Dale had crash-landed two months ago.

Inland, a few kilometers outside the city, was the Defense Research Center, which they headed for by groundcar after leaving Dale and Zarkov at the entrance to one of the subplanet shuttle stations.

In the time that they had been on this planet, they all had been busy learning the history and, in a small measure, the technology of the Citadel computer.

Built twenty thousand years ago, the machine was vast almost beyond comprehension, as was the knowledge it contained. And yet, as sophisticated as the computer was, it simply was not advanced enough to handle the threat from the other civilization's Citadel computer.

The Defense Center Research, from above ground looked very much like an ordinary, if quite small, space shuttle port with a large, flat, paved area and a few low buildings here and there. However, beneath the surface of the landing pod area, Sandra Debonshire assured Flash, was the main research and construction facility.

Here was a vast underground cavern filled with scout ships of varying sizes and shapes. Many were so oddly constructed that they were just barely recognizable as space vessels, while others were so conventional in appearance that they looked like ordinary Earth-design shuttle craft.

Van d'Hoef had regained consciousness before they were out of the city, but had given them no trouble on the trip out. He stared morosely out the windscreen, as Flash sat in the seat behind him, ready for any trouble, with Sandra in the left seat at the controls.

Without hesitation she turned the groundcar into a ramp entrance and at breakneck speed descended into the research and construction facility.

"What are you going to do?" Van d'Hoef asked, finally breaking the silence.

The young woman didn't answer him; instead she concentrated on her driving.

The vast cavern was at least several kilometers long but no more than a couple of hundred meters below ground. Maintenance droids seemed to be everywhere, working in and on the various craft.

"Aren't the droids in contact with the main computer?" Flash asked as they neared the bottom of the spiral ramp.

Sandra glanced over her shoulder at him. "Yes, but only in a limited, very specific interface. They don't have external sensors in the usual meaning of the term. As long as we keep out of their way, we'll go undetected."

"You're going through with this insane stunt then?" Van d'Hoef said, his voice shrill.

"Yes, Peter," Sandra said wearily. "It's our only hope."

They had reached the bottom of the ramp, and the young woman parked the groundcar to one side, away from where a half-dozen droids were working on one of the scout ships. She climbed out of the low car, and Van d'Hoef started to get out, but Flash put a hand on his shoulder and pulled him back.

"No trouble," Flash said.

Van d'Hoef turned to look at Flash. His eyes were wild, and a thin bead of perspiration had formed on his upper lip. "Why are you determined to do this?"

"It's the only way we're going to get out of this in one piece."

Van d'Hoef's face screwed up into a grimace. "Do you honestly think you know more than the creators?"

"They built the machines, not us. And despite their vast intelligence they could not keep out of a war that lasted eighty thousand years."

"A war that's still going on," Van d'Hoef snapped.

"Yes," Flash said grimly. The two men looked at each other for a long time, neither fathoming the other's reasoning, until finally Flash let Van d'Hoef out of the car.

Sandra was looking around the cavern, obviously searching for something, and when Flash climbed out of the groundcar, she pointed. "There," she said excitedly.

Flash looked that way toward a large, oddly shaped craft that rose above the others around it, at least a half-kilometer away.

"It's the ship Martin used to transport us from the Goodhope. I'd hoped it would still be here."

"We don't need anything that big," Flash said.

"It's the only one I know of that's equipped with weapons."

Van d'Hoef had backed away from them, the wild look coming more intensely into his eyes. "No," he cried. "This is insanity!"

Before Flash could stop him, he scooted around the groundcar and, in a dead run, headed for the nearest droid, a half-dozen meters away.

Flash managed only to take a couple of steps after him before Van d'Hoef grabbed a metal bar from a roll-about cart and, swinging it like a club, smashed in the head of the maintenance droid, which went down in a heap.

Sirens sounded almost instantly, and from every corner of the huge depot, maintenance droids began converging on them.

Van d'Hoef leaped to the scout ship, less than a meter from the downed robot, and began hacking at it, the metal bar clanging off its side.

Flash was behind him in a few quick strides. As Van d'Hoef brought the bar back for another swing, Flash grabbed it out of his hands and spun the man around, sending him slamming into the scout ship.

"Flash!" Sandra screamed.

Flash turned in time to see two of the maintenance droids almost on top of him. Instinctively he stepped to one side, and using the metal bar just like Van d'Hoef had, smashed in their heads, knocking them backward.

More sirens sounded, other androids ran toward them, and the lights began to dim in the huge cavern as the main entry ramp doors silently slid shut.

Van d'Hoef had shrunk back against the side of the small scout ship and had fallen to his knees where he buried his face in his hands and sobbed.

Flash yanked the man to his feet, slung him over his shoulder, and, following Sandra, headed in a dead run for the bigger ship a half-kilometer distant.

One way or another they were going to have to warn Dr. Zarkov and Dale. If the main computer connected their actions at the computer control center with what was happening here in the research depot, there could be more trouble than any of them could handle.

Sandra was about ten meters ahead of Flash when she went around one of the scout ships. A moment later he came around the corner, and he pulled up short. She was gone.

He took a couple of steps to the left so that he could peer around the edge of another ship, and from where he stood he had a clear view down a narrow aisle to the vessel they were headed for, still a long way off. Yet the young woman was nowhere in sight.

Something behind him caught Flash's attention, and he started to turn around when something slammed into the back of his head. A blackness seemed to envelop him as he watched, amazed, that the floor was coming up to meet his face, Van d'Hoef still slung over his shoulder.

The computer run had been streaming data into a shunted comparator memory circuit for nearly ten hours without results, when Zarkov straightened up from where he had been hunched over a terminal. He stretched, then shuffled around the main console to where Dale lay curled up in a contour chair, sound asleep.

For several long moments he stood, silently looking down at her, and a wave of love for his niece washed through him.

The two months they had been here had been hard on her in more than one way, he knew. Besides the fact that she missed the normal social intercourse with friends back on Earth, there was the business with Flash.

Zarkov felt like a Federation arbitrator, able to clearly see both sides of the issue. And yet he was unable to say or do anything about his findings without becoming a meddling old man.

Dale was deeply in love with Flash. That was obvious, had been obvious for years now. At first, when Flash's wife, Doris, was still alive, Zarkov had worried about his young niece, hoping against hope that what she felt for Flash was nothing more than a young woman's infatuation.

But as time passed, and Dale's love deepened as she matured, his worry turned into near-terror. She was killing herself by slow degrees, loving a man who was deeply committed to another woman.

And then the unthinkable happened. Doris had been brutally murdered. And Zarkov had watched the terrible conflict raging within his niece. Then too he had understood, and yet had been able to say nothing.

She loved Flash deeply, and one part of her desperately wanted to bring his wife back to life so that the man would not be so unhappy, so crushed, so unfulfilled. And yet another part of Dale, a part she was unaware that her uncle could see, was secretly glad that Flash was free.

That feeling in itself had set up a deep-seated guilt complex in Dale, a guilt that at times he wondered if his niece could handle.

But time continued to pass. Flash's memory of his wife began to fade, the raw edges began to dull, and Dale's hope of someday becoming Mrs. Gordon rose.

Here now on Citadel, completely isolated from Earth, from their usual day-to-day routine, Dale had expected Flash to come to her. Yet he had not.

Finally, however, it seemed to Zarkov that his niece was beginning to understand that Flash perhaps was not for her, possibly would never be hers. It seemed that she was finally coming to accept that. But at what cost, he wondered.

"Have we got an answer yet?" Dale asked.

Zarkov was jerked out of his thoughts, and he focused on Dale, who was looking up at him, sleep still clouding her eyes. He shook his head.

"Not yet," he said. "I'm sorry if I woke you."

She stretched luxuriously and then got up from the couch to peck him on the cheek. "Why don't you get some sleep?" she said. "I'll keep watch on the terminal for a while."

He shook his head absently. "I've set up a random pattern search that has to be constantly monitored. If we went at it in any logical manner, we could be here a hundred years or more."

"Come on and show me how it works," Dale said, taking her uncle's arm and leading him back around the console to the one data terminal that he had set up for their search. "You can't go without sleep all night."

Back at the terminal, streams of data flashed across the screen in double matrix arrays. He watched the units of information for a few moments and then reached out and punched a button that froze the data stream.

Two cubicle arrays of numbers and symbols were displayed side by side on the screen, and Zarkov pointed to the one on the left. "I've set up a fairly narrow probability model of what the home system must be like. Working backward from what knowledge the computer had about the physiology and psychology of the builders of the Citadel, I came up with a number of prerequisites for the Centrus system. Star type, size and color, planetary configuration and distance from the central star, a single moon near Earth normal—some of their literature discussed tides and tidal influence as a fairly uncomplicated subject—and the copper-granite-based composition instead of iron-based."

Dale leaned forward and studied the left matrix for a long moment, able to pick out the symbols for most of what her uncle had explained.

He continued. "Then, working with the rather

loose assumption that the Centrus system is located somewhere within a thousand-light-year radius of the exact galactic center, I had the computer set up a random search pattern of all stars, eliminating immediately the obviously useless choices—binaries, red giants, white dwarfs, and the like. But in a random pattern. A star or two here, a star or two there."

Dale was shaking her head. "That wouldn't work unless the computer had in its data banks the coordinates for the Centrus system. Perhaps the builders omitted all references to the home system."

Zarkov smiled. "I thought of that, so I based my search on a recent star scan toward the galactic center. I'm basing my search on new information—post-creation information, if you will."

Suddenly understanding dawned on Dale's face. "Every time the computer comes up with a star system that could fit your prediction of what the Centrus system must be like, you query the computer for more detailed information."

Zarkov again smiled and nodded. "The system that the computer cannot or will not tell us about will probably be Centrus."

"You're trusting the computer to give you an accurate scan. Maybe the stellar system picture it took for you has the Centrus system automatically blocked out."

"Not possible, at least it's not possible if Martin was telling us the truth about hyperjump points. He says the Citadel can and does build ships that do not need catalogued hyperpoints as such. At any point in space, a hyperjump can be made. That means every single body of any significant gravitational influence in the galaxy has to be precatalogued. It's the only way hyperdrive jumps can be made with any assurance of reasonable accuracy. So my search simply becomes a comparison between what the computer scanned for me and what the computer will tell me. The comparison should reveal the single system that exists, but that the computer can't say anything about."

Zarkov reached out again and punched the run button, and the computer continued its random search.

For several minutes Dale remained by her uncle's side, watching the progress of the search. From time to time a stellar system would match his model and he would quickly punch the stop program and comparator start buttons, then query the computer for more information on that particular system. Each time, however, the computer would respond with a wealth of data, Zarkov would shrug and calmly punch the comparator stop and program run buttons, and the search would continue.

"What's the chance of finding the right system within the next ten hours?" she asked finally.

Zarkov glanced at his niece. "I've played with the problem off and on, but I think there's no way of assigning any realistic probability. We'll either get lucky or we won't."

"Are you sure you don't want me to work the program for a while, uncle?"

He shook his head. "Maybe later. The run is starting to drift into the galactic core area, and I think I'll hold it there for a while. Some of their literature talked about brightly lit evenings. Could be an indication of a high concentration of stars in the night sky, which would be more likely at the exact galactic center."

She turned away and went to the far end of the console where the matter transmitter portal controls were located along with the planetwide communications console. Among the first things they had done when they came down here shortly after noon was to close off the portal for this center and set up the coordinates for their transmission to the highway outside the city where they were supposed to meet Flash and Sandra. But Dale had also set up a query monitor on the communications board that would indicate anyone trying to make contact with them down here.

As she passed the end of the console she glanced that way and stopped in midstride, her heart skipping a beat. The communications board was lit up like a Christmas holograph.

"Uncle!" she cried out, rushing to the console. She punched one of the communication channel buttons, and Philip Redmann, one of the Goodhope technicians who had worked with Zarkov on the computer control center, came on the visiscreen.

"Dr. Zarkov, thank God . . . ," he started, but when he saw it was Dale at the console, he stopped. "Miss Arden?" he said.

"Good evening, Philip," Dale replied, trying as best she could to keep her voice and facial expression normal. "Did you want to speak to my uncle?"

The man seemed upset. "Something has happened," he said. "Martin has . . . disappeared. And so has Col. Gordon, and Sandy. We thought they were with you."

Dale shook her head. "No," she said. "My uncle and I are down here alone. We're continuing with the control center retrofit."

Redmann seemed even more agitated. "What's going on?" he sputtered. "I mean, we were having a meeting and all of a sudden you all disappeared. We can't even find Capt. Van d'Hoef."

"Find Martin," Dale said evenly. "I'm sure he'll explain everything." She paused a moment, but before Redmann could object she continued. "We're a little busy down here just now, Phil, but you can do me a favor."

"Favor?" Redmann asked, even more confused than before.

"As a matter of fact, two favors. First of all, as soon as you find Martin, have him call me down here. Can you do that?"

"Sure . . . ," Redmann stammered.

"And I can see that my communications board is lit up. I'm sure some of the others are looking for us. Explain everything to them like a sweetheart, will you?"

"I . . . ," Redmann started, but Dale did not let him finish.

"Thanks Phil, you're a dear . . . bye." She reached out and punched the cancel query control, and the board went dead.

Flash and Sandra had said they were going to the Defense Research Center. Sooner or later someone from the Goodhope's crew would look there. She would have to warn them. She queried the computer for the center's coordinates, then punched the numbers into the communication board.

The visiscreen shimmered a moment, then the image cleared at the center's communications console. No one was there.

"Flash?" Dale called. "Sandra?"

There was no answer, and she was about to call again when Dr. Zarkov came from the other end of the console, out of breath and more excited than she had ever seen him before.

"We've done it," he was saying. "We've found it."

She turned to him. "Uncle?" she said, confused.

"The Centrus coordinates—I've found them!"

"Flash is in trouble," she said, barely hearing or understanding what her uncle was saying. "We've got to go to him."

At that moment Sandra was on the visiscreen. "Dale?" she shouted.

Dale swiveled around toward the console, in time to see Sandra turn away from the screen for a moment and then turn back. Tears were streaming down the young woman's cheeks, and she looked pale.

"What is it?" Dale screamed. "What's happening?"

"It's Flash," Sandra shouted hysterically. "He's dead!"

CHAPTER 4

Sandra Debonshire broke the connection on the communications channel with a distraught Dale Arden, turned and snapped off a quick shot at an approaching maintenance droid with her .45 caliber automatic, then rushed back to the large shuttle ship.

Halfway up the ramp she stopped and turned back, scanning the area near the communications station, but nothing moved in the vicinity.

Across the research depot a number of warrior droids were moving into view, and Sandra shifted her weight nervously from one foot to the other.

"Come on," she said half to herself. "Hurry up . . ."

Her eyes darted back and forth between the advancing warrior droids, still a long way off, and the area of the communications station.

Suddenly the air in front of the console began to shimmer and dance with a million tiny spots of light, as Dale Arden and her uncle materialized from the data control center.

When the transference was complete, Dale looked up, confused. Then she spotted Sandra, and she gave out a little cry and rushed forward, her uncle following directly behind her.

"Did you get the coordinates?" Sandra shouted.

"Flash!" Dale screamed. "Where is he?" She started up the ramp, but behind her Zarkov stumbled and fell to his knees as a maintenance droid appeared from around the corner of a nearby scout ship.

Sandra took a couple of steps down the ramp, brushing Dale's outstretched hands away, and fired two shots, the heavy gun bucking in her hand.

The maintenance droid, which had nearly reached Zarkov, stepped backward, a spurt of hydrodynamic fluid spraying from its torso like blood from a human being, and amid a shower of sparks, it crumpled in a heap.

Sandra was off the ramp in two steps and at Zarkov's side, where she unceremoniously dragged the old man to his feet and hauled him up the ramp.

"Move!" she screamed at Dale, who turned, crying, and stumbled up the ramp into the ship.

Once inside, Sandra turned and hit a control, and the ramp half-folded on itself and pivoted up, sealing off the entrance. A sigh of air caused their ears to pop as the ship automatically pressurized.

"What about Flash?" Dale screeched, still hysterical. "My God . . . take me to him, Sandra."

Sandra stuffed the automatic into a hip pocket of her white coveralls and took both of Dale's hands in hers. For a moment their eyes were locked together. "Now listen to me, Dale. You've got to get ahold of yourself."

"Flash . . . ," Dale cried.

"Flash is hurt, but he'll be all right."

"But you said he was . . . dead . . . you told me he was dead!" Dale's voice had risen even higher in pitch.

"I lied for the computer's benefit."

Zarkov had caught his breath. "What happened?" he asked. "Where is he?"

Sandra turned to him. "He's on board. Once we get out of here, I'll take you to him."

"Now!" Dale screamed.

"Did you get the Centrus coordinates?" Sandra asked Zarkov, ignoring Dale's continued frenzy.

Zarkov nodded uncertainly, not knowing whether to comfort Dale or cooperate with Sandra. "Yes, I have them," he finally answered.

"Thank God," Sandra said. "We've got to get out of here right now." She took Zarkov by the arm, turned, and led him and Dale, who was on the verge of collapse, down a narrow passageway lined with various lights, dials, grilles, tubing, and wiring.

Through a hatch they came into a large, circular room, the walls of which contained a hundred or more acceleration couches swung on gimbals.

Without hesitation Sandra led them across the room, up a narrow ramp, and through a smaller circular hatch where they found themselves on the bridge of the ship.

There were several deeply padded acceleration couches, each in front of an equipment console, all of them facing the forward viewscreens.

Sandra helped Zarkov strap into one of the couches. "This is a fairly simple astrogation tank. Once I get us out of here, I want you to set up the jump with the Centrus coordinates. The hyper-point feed-ins are all automatic. You won't have to scan."

Zarkov nodded his understanding, and Sandra turned to Dale and shook her head. "You're not going to be much help, are you?"

Tears were streaming down Dale's eyes. "I've got to see him first."

Sandra nodded in the direction they had come from. "Back through the hatch, then take the ramp up to the right. He and Peter are there. I'll give you one minute to strap down, and then we're lifting off."

Without waiting to hear more, Dale turned and rushed off the bridge. Sandra strapped herself into the acceleration couch at the command module and began hitting buttons and controls pre-paratory to taking off.

The bridge came alive with various indicator lights and dozens of data terminals displaying in-formation, and from somewhere below them a low-pitched rumbling began as the reaction engines started to warm up.

"How did you learn to run this ship?" Zarkov called out to her.

"Coming up on V sub M, ready for onboard in-terface," Sandra spoke into her command module. She turned to look over her shoulder. "This is the ship I used to return to the Goodhope," she said softly.

"Oh," Zarkov said, and he went back to his work, feeding the coordinates for the Centrus system into the astrogation tank.

"Assuming manual control," Sandra told the onboard sequencing computer, and a chime sounded as the board went green.

She reached out and punched the ship's intercom and siren buttons. "Strap down, Dale, we're lifting off. Now!"

A moment later she hit the engine gates and slowly cranked up the power with her right hand, while with her left she hit the control for the overhead research depot doors.

The forward viewscreens came alive, and Sandra looked up as the ship began to rise away from the depot floor toward the ceiling a hundred meters overhead, which was beginning to slide open. She breathed a sigh of relief.

For the moment, at least, the computer was confused and was doing nothing to prevent their departure. Martin was missing. Dale and Dr. Zarkov had been tampering with Data Control. Van d'Hoef had destroyed a maintenance droid and had tried to damage a scout ship. Flash had stopped Van d'Hoef, but then had destroyed two droids himself, and as far as the computer knew, he was now dead, killed by still another droid.

On top of all that, Sandra Debonshire was leaving the research depot with the shuttle ship that had been used to transport the Goodhope's crew to the Citadel.

But the computer's inaction would not last much longer, she knew. Although the machine had no intuitive circuitry, its correlative functions were highly refined. Soon, very soon, it would evaluate all the facts, discovering the threat to the Citadel's existence, and would attempt to stop them.

Accelerating, the large shuttle vessel cleared the depot ceiling opening, and a moment later flashed up into the night sky toward an escape orbit, the city below them receding until it was nothing more than a dim glow next to the vast, dark sea.

For a moment everything in the past came back to Sandra. The awakening on Citadel I, with the droid Martin tending to them. The first days of explanations, the following weeks and months of preparations, and then the unthinkable. Back into space. Coming aboard the Goodhope. Seeing her friends, her fellow crewmates, lying peacefully asleep. And killing them, knowing paradoxically that they were alive and safe back on Citadel I, allowing her to do what she had to do; yet she was mutilating, horribly mutilating, their bodies. Slashing and cutting, on and on, thinking that it would continue forever. And then her own body.

The communications board chimed, and Sandra opened the channel.

"Sandra Debonshire," a soft, sonorous man's voice said. It was the voice of Citadel I. She had heard it only once before, fifty years ago.

A jump into hyperspace could be made safely only in as complete a vacuum as possible, which meant that they had to be at least five thousand kilometers above the planet's surface if they were to have any margin of safety whatsoever. And even at that distance, dust particles and stray molecules of oxygen or other gas might leak from the planet's atmosphere into space, destroying that vacuum.

Sandra's eyes glanced from the doppler radar, which showed their distance from the planet's surface, to the communications board. They needed more time.

She closed the communications channel for a moment and turned toward Zarkov. "At five thousand kilometers, hit the hyperdrive."

"It's too close," Zarkov said, alarmed.

"We'll never get out of here if we wait any longer than that," she shouted urgently. "The machine will put a tractor beam on us any second."

Without waiting for Zarkov's reply, she turned back and reopened the communications channel. "What do you want?" she said.

"What have you done with Martin?" the Citadel computer asked. The question surprised her.

The planet's curvature was evident at this height, and through the forward viewscreen she could see the terminator area between daylight and night far to the east.

"I don't know what you're talking about," she said. She glanced again at the doppler radar. Too soon. Too soon!

"I want you to return so that we can help you, Sandra. I want to help Col. Gordon as well."

The stars shone as hard, brilliant points against a totally black sky, and in the direction of the sun the forward viewscreen had automatically darkened, blocking out the harsh, ultraviolet radiation. The ship was accelerating steadily.

"All right," Sandra said slowly, defeat strong in her voice.

"Shut down your engines now, Sandra, and I will help you return home."

"Just a moment," she said. It was too soon. Her board began going red, and their rate of acceleration was slowing down. It had to be now!

"Now!" she shouted to Zarkov.

Zarkov hesitated a moment, and Sandra began frantically struggling with the straps that held her down. Finally, however, he reached out and, with a shaking hand, hit the hyperdrive activate control.

"You must not . . . ," the voice of the Citadel computer said, and then it was cut off as wave after wave of nausea and dizziness swept through Sandra's body. The stars visible through the forward viewscreen seemed to blossom and streak the sky, ranging through the spectrum, changing colors from red to yellow to blue, and suddenly they were gone.

Music seemed to be playing from somewhere in the distance, and Flash Gordon thought it strange that his head should hurt so badly because of it. He opened his eyes after a long moment and squinted against the brightness of the light, up into someone's face. For a moment he could neither recognize the person standing over him nor put a name to her. Her!

"Dale," he said, suddenly struggling to sit up as everything rushed into place.

Dale gently pushed him back down on the automed couch, bent down, and brushed her lips against his forehead. When she straightened up there were tears in her eyes.

"What happened?" he said, raising his right hand to his throbbing head.

"You gave us a big scare, that's what happened," Dale said, and he could hear the relief in her voice. She reached behind him and flipped a switch. "He's come around finally," she said.

"How is he?" another woman's voice asked from over an intercom speaker.

Dale looked down at Flash and managed a slight, harried smile. "He looks terrible, but the automed says he's fine."

"We're nailing everything down up here— shouldn't take more than a couple of minutes. When we're finished we'll join you."

Dale flipped the intercom off. "How do you feel, Flash?"

"Like I've been hit with a battering ram," he said. Every muscle in his body ached, and his head throbbed so badly it seemed as if it would explode at any minute.

"The machine says you had a slight concussion, but other than that you should be fine. Pulse normal, temperature exactly where it should be, and only a slightly elevated blood pressure."

Flash slowly sat up and swung his legs over the edge of the medical couch. A wave of dizziness washed over him.

Dale helped him steady himself on the edge of the couch until the feeling passed. Then he looked up and around the small room that was equipped with a half-dozen other similar couches with large control consoles of some kind behind each one.

Van d'Hoef was lying on the couch next to his, and he glared up at Flash and Dale.

"Good morning," Flash said to him, but Van d'Hoef turned his head the other way, hate shining deeply in his eyes.

"He's been like that ever since Uncle Hans and I came up from Data Control," Dale said. She shuddered. "I thought you were dead," she said, looking at Flash with wonder in her eyes.

"Where are we?" he asked.

"In hyperspace," Dale answered, looking closely at him. "Are you sure you're all right?"

"Sore, but functioning," Flash said. He raised his right hand and with his fingertips gently touched a spot at the back of his head, and then he winced as pain seared his brain. He remembered running toward the large shuttle vessel, Van d'Hoef slung over his shoulder, and he had lost sight of Sandra. He also remembered thinking that someone or something was coming up behind him. Then, nothing.

"I see Col. Gordon has decided to join the living," Sandra said, coming into the medical station. Zarkov was right behind her. He looked worried.

Flash looked up. "How did you manage alone?" he asked.

She laughed out loud. "It wasn't easy. You've got a mass of at least a hundred kilos, maybe more. I've never lifted anything so heavy in all my life."

Deep concern was written over Zarkov's features, mixed with a look of weariness. "How are you feeling now, Flash?" he asked.

"Better," Flash said. "But hungry. And it looks as if you could use some rest."

"We all could," Sandra said, and she and Dale helped Flash off the couch. Together the four of them went back down the ramp into the ship's main cabin, where they sat around a large circular table. No one had mentioned Van d'Hoef, and the man had not moved from where he lay when they left.

While Sandra began pulling various containers of food and drink from the autochef in the bulkhead next to the table, Flash looked around the room, which was mostly filled with acceleration couches, their straps hanging loose.

"This was the ship Martin used to bring the Goodhope's crew back to the Citadel, wasn't it?" he said.

"Yes," Sandra answered, laying out the food containers on the table. She brushed a strand of sand-blonde hair from her forehead. "I also used this ship to return to the Goodhope. It's one of the reasons I took it. I was trained in its systems."

Flash looked sharply at Zarkov. "You found the coordinates for the Centrus system?"

Zarkov nodded. "We're on our way, but the computer tried to stop us."

"Then we can't return," Flash said half to himself. When he looked up the others were staring at him. "How long was I out?"

"Eleven hours," Sandra said. She had brought the last of the food and drink to the table, and she sat down and poured Flash a cup of coffee. The aroma instantly filled the room, and Flash sipped at the hot liquid. It tasted wonderful.

"One of the maintenance droids came up behind you and struck you in the back of the head with its torsional appendage. You went down. I thought you were dead and started screaming." Sandra looked sheepishly at Flash. "The central computer evidently thought so too, because the maintenance droid's sentient circuits all blew, and everything in the research depot came to a halt long enough for me to drag you and Peter into the ship and strap you both into the automed. First, though, I disconnected your automed feed, which would have connected you with the main computer, and set up some bogus readings. All zeros."

"So the computer did believe I was dead, and yet you were apparently trying with the automed to revive me."

"Exactly," Sandra said. "It gave me enough time to redo at least the command and astrogation tank modules on the bridge, so that if and when we were able to leave, the computer would have no direct control over us."

"That's why you told me he was dead," Dale said.

Sandra turned to look at her. "I'm sorry I had to do that to you, Dale, but it was the only way to get you here without arousing too much suspicion in the computer's correlative circuitry."

"It worked," Dale said. "I believed you."

"How did you know I had come up with the Centrus coordinates?" Zarkov asked, sitting forward. The old man was dead tired and barely able to keep his eyes open.

"I didn't," Sandra said, shaking her head. "But it had been ten hours since Flash had been put out of commission, and the computer had sent down a half-dozen warrior robots to find out what was going on. With or without the coordinates we had to get out of there, and fast."

"You said the computer tried to stop us?" Flash asked.

Sandra turned back to him and nodded. "It

asked me to come back, and at the last moment it put a tractor beam on us. At that instant we went into hyperspace."

"At 4,800 kilometers out," Zarkov added.

Flash whistled. "That was cutting it close," he said.

"You slept through it all," Sandra said, and they all laughed, the quip easing everyone's tension.

"I'm curious about one other thing," Zarkov said after a moment.

"Yes?" Sandra said pleasantly. None of them wanted to think about Centrus and what they would find there. At least not until later.

"The weapon you used. It seemed to be firing a projectile."

"It's called a .45 caliber automatic," Van d'Hoef's high-pitched voice shrilled from behind them, and they all snapped around in their seats in time to see the man come down the ramp from the medical station. He was holding one of the weapons in his right hand. "Standard equipment aboard the Goodhope two hundred years ago. Sandra was thoughtful enough at the time to bring some of our things with her."

"Peter," Sandra said, half-rising from her chair.

"Sit down, Sandra, or I will kill you now instead of later," Van d'Hoef said. There was a maniacal expression on his face.

"What do you want?" Flash asked. He had pushed his chair slightly away from the table, and he gauged the distance between him and Van d'Hoef. But it was too far. He'd never make it.

"We're going home."

"We can't go back," Sandra said. "The computer would never allow it."

"I don't mean to the Citadel. I mean home. Earth."

They were all stunned. "Why?" Sandra asked.

"With this ship and what I've learned from the computer over the past 120 years, I could lead an expedition back to take over the Citadel. It wouldn't be easy, but it could be done. And I'd lead it."

"No," Sandra said, half-rising again.

"Sit down!" Van d'Hoef shouted, and she once again sunk down. "Dr. Zarkov is going to program the astrogation tank with Earth's coordinates. Immediately."

"I won't do it," Zarkov said, sitting back.

Van d'Hoef laughed and raised the automatic so that it was pointed directly at Dale. "If you won't cooperate, Doctor, your niece will be the first to die."

CHAPTER 5

A tremendous explosion hammered against the walls of the main cabin, and Van d'Hoef was flung backward. A dark hole appeared in his chest, spreading an angry red stain down the front of his white coveralls.

Instantly Flash leaped up and slammed Dale off her chair into a heap beneath the table. But Van d'Hoef was no longer a threat.

Flash slowly got to his feet in time to see Sandra lay her .45 automatic on the table. Her hands were shaking and her complexion had turned a deathly white.

She looked up at Flash, absolute defeat and dejection in her eyes. "There wasn't anything else for me to do," she said in a hoarse voice. "You see that, don't you?"

Dale picked herself up from the deck, and her eyes darted from Sandra to the bloody heap that had been Van d'Hoef.

"He didn't know I had the gun in my pocket. And I could see that the safety on his gun hadn't been clicked off. But he would have killed us all. Oh God ...," the young woman wailed, and she buried her face in her hands.

Dale came around the table and sat beside Sandra, holding her shoulders as the young woman wept.

"She loved him," Dale said, looking up at Flash. "She told me that five weeks ago."

Flash shook his head, then turned to Zarkov. "Are you all right, Doc?"

Zarkov nodded. He too had turned white. "Maybe there's something the automed can do for him," he said, indicating Van d'Hoef.

Flash turned and went across the room to where Van d'Hoef's body lay crumpled against the base of one of the acceleration couches. His eyes were open and he wasn't breathing. Flash bent down and gently turned the man over, then almost recoiled. The weapon's projectile had made a fair-size hole in his chest but had blasted a ragged opening at least a dozen centimeters wide in his back. The man was dead—there was no doubt about it. And the damage to his body was so massive that no automed in the universe could help now.

Zarkov got up and came across the room. Flash looked up at him and shook his head. "It's no use," he said.

"Barbaric," Zarkov said softly, but with much emotion in his voice. He turned away from the grisly sight and looked at Dale and Sandra. He shook his head. "Barbaric," he repeated. "A hundred and fifty-eight people were murdered aboard the Goodhope. And now this man. Casualties of a war that has lasted thousands of years. When will it end?"

"Perhaps never," Flash said, getting wearily to his feet. His head was throbbing worse than before, and he was beginning to see double.

If the war continued, how could they expect to end it, or even in a small way have any effect on its course? Two young women, a banged-up Federation Central Intelligence Division colonel, and an old man—a brilliant scientist, but an old man nevertheless—were pitting themselves against a computer technology far beyond their knowledge.

"How long before insertion to the Centrus system?" he asked Zarkov after a moment.

The aging scientist turned to him. "A week," he shrugged. "Maybe a day or so more. It's hard to pinpoint the relative passage of time in hyperdrive, especially with equipment I'm not familiar with."

"We'll need a week," Flash said. "At least that." He turned back to Van d'Hoef's body, bent down, and with some difficulty, because of his head injury, picked the man up and headed toward the aft airlock. The body would be dragged along outside the ship in warp until they came out of hyperdrive, when it would break loose. When he was finished with this grisly task, he was going to turn himself over to the automed and then sleep, perhaps for the entire week if he could get away with it.

The Citadel I transport class shuttle vessel came out of hyperspace one million kilometers from the third planet of the system Dr. Zarkov had identified as Centrus, the seat of the once-powerful galactic civilization.

As the ship's reaction engines braked against the

tremendous velocity they had come out of hyper-space with, a huge corona appeared, flaming be-hind them at least ten thousand kilometers, and the area of space in their vicinity came awesomely alive.

They had materialized into real space in an area very near the center of the galaxy where the con-centration of stars was much higher than around the rim worlds such as Earth. On any one of the Centrus system planets, they all realized, there could never be anything like night as they knew it from Earth or Citadel I. There were simply too many stars. The effect, Dr. Zarkov told them, would be like a thousand bands of Milky Ways fill-ing the night sky. Many of the stars would even be visible during the day.

Zarkov, Dale, Sandra, and Flash were on the bridge of the shuttle vessel, staring gape-mouthed at the spectacle, when a chime sounded from one of the electromagnetic scanners.

They all looked up as Sandra hit the search and identify button, and the data terminal instantly identified the signal.

"It's a homing beacon," she said, awed. "Com-ing from the third planet."

Flash swiveled his overhead module in place and brought the beacon up on the data terminal, his orbital insertion computer confirming what Sandra had told them.

It was a homing beacon—weak, but definitely a beacon.

"Is there someone still alive down there?" Dale asked in a hushed tone.

The effect of the dense stellar patterns along with

the beacon itself had somewhat intimidated them all.

"I don't think so," Zarkov said. He too had brought the beacon up on his terminal, and he had sent out a ship-to-ground installation query with no response. He looked up and caught Flash's eye. "The beacon is twenty thousand years old at least, and yet it's still functioning. Unbelievable."

"Are we going to follow it in?" Flash asked.

Zarkov chewed at his lower lip a moment, a gesture he unconsciously made whenever he was pondering some difficult decision. He glanced back at the monitor terminal, then looked again at Flash. "We'll watch the beacon for any sign of an identifying query. This was a planet at war. I would assume they would have defenses that would automatically be activated against any approaching vessel that could not identify itself as friendly."

Flash nodded. "I don't think I'd care to be fired at with automatic weapons built by engineers who could construct a continually operating beacon that is still functioning after twenty thousand years."

"No," Zarkov said, and they all fell silent as they watched the third planet grow in their forward viewscreens from a tiny speck into a blue and brown globe very reminiscent of Earth.

A great southern sea, dotted with numerous islands, seemed to take up at least half the planet's surface. At the southern tip of the mainland mass they could identify what appeared to be a widespread tropical storm.

"Some of the planet's systems have broken down," Sandra commented. "They had weather

control, so such storms would not have existed
when the city was functioning." There was deep
disappointment in her voice, and Flash knew exactly what she was driving at.

"If there is a data bank, it would be the most
protected of any of Centrus's systems," he said.
"The beacon is still working, so there's a very good
chance the data bank will be functional as well."

"I hope so," Sandra said, turning to glance at
him.

The plasma engines of the shuttle craft kicked in
for suborbital flight, and Flash watched over
Sandra's shoulder as she skillfully brought the ship
into the planet's outer atmosphere on manual control, riding the beacon down, keeping the target
dot exactly centered on the ship's line-of-position
indicator.

The beacon was leading them toward the southern end of the land mass, directly to the middle of
the huge storm, and as high as twenty thousand
meters they began encountering turbulence that
caused the big ship to pitch and yaw despite the
sophisticated gyro systems.

"We'd better strap down," Flash said, and as
they all tightened their harnesses the turbulence in-
creased. A high-pitched whine seemed to shudder
throughout the ship from the atmosphere's drag on
the hull.

Sandra had flipped on her sequencing computer
and was rapidly speaking into the pickup on her
command module.

"Coming up on V sub M and holding," she said.

Dale was staring out the forward viewscreens,
while Zarkov continued to watch for any challenge

from the beacon signal and Flash had activated his own overhead to follow the rapidly changing displays. Sandra brought them lower into the atmosphere, and their velocity began to bleed off.

"One-five-oh K and mark," Sandra spoke into the computer pickup. "Plasma drive override." She reached up and flipped two switches activating the ship's gravity-resist generator, and Flash's stomach flopped over as the device came on line, but instantly their progress through the upper cloud layers smoothed out.

A chime sounded on the overhead, and Zarkov snapped around. "We've got a warble on the beacon," he said. "It looks like some kind of a tractor beam approach system."

"Override beacon guidance," Sandra spoke smoothly into the computer. "Regaining manual control and navigation."

Without being told, Flash reached up and switched control of the ship to his console. "I've got it," he said to Sandra, and she instantly took over navigation duties from the beacon monitor itself.

"Seventy-five K and mark," Flash told the sequencing computer, reading the numbers directly from the doppler radar. On more sophisticated ships, even vessels the Federation was building, sequencing for takeoffs and landings was often done by Guardian computers. But on shuttle vessels such systems were never installed, not even on Citadel I shuttle vessels. Additionally, this vessel had been designed for use by the droid Martin, who himself was a highly sophisticated computer system.

"On the beam," Sandra called out. "Coming up on V sub M-two. Mark one."

"Mark one," Flash repeated, and he eased back on the plasma drive units, causing their rate of descent to slow as they came deeper into the atmospheric storm. In the background he could hear the gravity-resist generators begin to whine toward overload, and he kept ready to assume total manual control, even against the turbulence. The ship's systems had never been meant for use in any kind of prolonged atmospheric storm. It was primarily a deep space shuttle.

"Fifty K and mark," Flash told the computer as they passed the five thousand meter level, and the gravity-resist generators began screaming like a strong wind through an open tower.

On a lower control board, Flash cranked up a set of infrared filters and scanner on the main forward viewscreen. Instantly the land mass directly below them was outlined in a strange blue, the warmer layers of atmosphere in contrasting reds.

"Hang on," Flash shouted over the rising noise. "Going manual." He leaned forward, and with his head against the cushioned scanning screen hood, he reached up and flipped off the gravity-resist generators. The vessel was violently slammed to one side, its stabilizing electromagnetic gyro systems whining in protest.

For the next three minutes, which seemed to Flash almost like an eternity, he fought the ungainly ship down through the violent tropical storm, the beacon beam superimposed on his scanning screen, and their altitude numbers unreeling in the upper right-hand corner of the screen, until they were around a hundred meters above what appeared in Flash's scope to be a spaceport.

"Landing struts extended," Flash called out.

There was a whirring noise, and then four distinct thumps. "Board is green," Sandra called out.

At fifty meters above the surface, Flash looked up, flipped off the plasma drive units, and quickly played the gravity-resist generator aft control to bring them in for a smooth touchdown. Then he shut off the drive systems, sat back after a moment, and deeply sighed.

"We're down," he said, glad now that he had spent most of his time, after the automed had finished with him, studying the ship's systems.

Sandra flipped off the scanner from her console so that the forward viewscreens suddenly gave a clear, nonaugmented view of outside, and then she hit the audio pickup.

The sound of the shrieking wind, along with the rain pelting the hull, quickly filled the bridge, matching the blotted-out picture of the storm through the viewscreens.

She shut off the sound after a moment and turned to look over the edge of her seat at Flash. "Nice landing, Colonel," she said, smiling. "But I don't think we're going out in that. At least not at the moment."

Dale had an odd expression on her face that both Flash and Sandra caught. He was about to ask her if she was all right, when Zarkov looked up from his console. "I'm showing local gravity at point eight Citadel normal, with an atmospheric at eighty-five percent normal oxygen content."

"Which makes this planet quite a bit lighter than

Earth, with a very thin atmosphere." Flash added.

"It's within limits," Zarkov said. "The only thing we'll have to watch for is too high an ultraviolet exposure." He glanced back at his console. "Temperature out there at the moment is a comfortable twenty degrees celsius, but the wind is peaking at nearly two hundred kilometers per Earth standard hour."

"A hurricane," Dale said, and Zarkov nodded. "Sandra is right—we're not going out in that."

Flash unstrapped his harnesses and got up from his acceleration couch and stretched. He was somewhat tired from the strain of the landing, but the automed had done its work well on his body. He felt fit and ready to see whatever this planet had to offer, if anything. But they would have to remain cooped up in the ship for several hours, by the looks of the storm, so he decided he would spend those hours relaxing.

"Lunch anyone?" he asked in a flippant tone of voice.

Zarkov shook his head absently. "I'm going to start a lifeform scan immediately," he said.

Dale had unstrapped and had climbed out of her couch, but Sandra remained where she was seated.

"I'm going to start a filtered scan to see what I can come up with."

"What are you looking for?" Flash asked.

Sandra looked up at him and shrugged. "Radio noise. Gravity generator activity. Reaction engines. I don't know. Anything I can find."

"And if we find nothing other than the beacon?"

Sandra looked away. "I don't know," she said. "We can't go back to Citadel I. And I wouldn't fit back home."

Flash was about to make a comment, but he realized that there was nothing he could say or do at this moment that would give the young woman any comfort. She had pinned her hopes on finding something here on Centrus. The beacon itself was like a ray of hope. But it was possible that only the beacon remained. And if that was the case there would be nothing or no one for her anywhere in the galaxy.

Flash was faintly depressed as he followed Dale back into the main salon, and at first he didn't notice her preoccupation. He sat at the table, and Dale got coffee for both of them before she too took a seat.

Flash sipped at the hot liquid and let his mind wander for a moment. "I wonder why a ship designed for a robot had an autochef installed?"

"Bringing back the human crew of the Goodhope, I suppose," Dale said tonelessly.

Flash looked up out of his thoughts at her. There was something wrong. "What's the matter, Dale?"

She looked at him. "I don't know," she said. "That is, I don't know for sure. But something is screwy."

"With what?"

She shook her head. "Not with what, with whom. Sandra Debonshire. One minute Miss Helpless, the next Miss Efficient."

"Aren't you being a little hard on her?"

"I don't think so, Flash," Dale said, and she put her coffee cup down and leaned forward, her arms on the table. "One week ago she killed the man she told me she loved. And yet she hasn't mentioned a thing about it since. No remorse. No wishes that it could have worked out differently. No feeling sorry for Van d'Hoef, or for herself for that matter."

"She's blocked it out."

"No, it means nothing to her. She killed 157 of her crewmates, and then tossed her own body out an airlock. The act unbalanced her, she told us. What she had to do made Citadel's control of her imperfect."

"I don't understand," Flash started to say, but Dale cut him off.

"She's not unbalanced. If anything, she's more balanced at this moment than you and I put together. If anything, she's too balanced. But she's hiding something."

"Like what?" Flash said, but he was beginning to understand what Dale was trying to say. He had felt it back at Citadel, during Martin's meeting. And there were other things as well that simply did not add up. One of them was Martin and his supposed ability to hide his data stream from the main computer. Such an ability did not fit with his prime directives.

"I think Martin wanted us to escape. I think this trip to Centrus was engineered for us. I think Sandra is working for the computer."

"Why drag us into this?"

"Like Martin said, you were able to beat the Citadel II droid in testing by doing something unexpected. You made a good fight of it. Exciting, isn't it? Besides, Sandra and all the others are nothing more than biological droids. I wouldn't be a bit surprised if there was another Van d'Hoef droid back on Citadel."

Flash turned away. "The war continues."

"You bet," Dale said. "The war never stopped.

Don't be overly surprised if we find a couple of Citadel II ships coming after us here. Sandra told you this ship was the one she wanted to take because it was the only one with weapons. Did you stop to wonder why she needed weapons if we were going to do nothing more than find Centrus and explore it?"

"You and I and your uncle are a new factor Martin has maneuvered into this war," Flash said.

"Wouldn't it be funny if the hyperdrive generator we found aboard the Goodhope wasn't installed by the Citadel II but was installed by Martin in order to snag some human beings? Some sentient beings with intuitive reasoning powers?"

Flash sat back. "Still, this is Centrus. And as long as we're able, we'll do what we set out to do. Maybe we'll become more effective weapons than Martin ever dreamed."

CHAPTER 6

It wasn't until the morning of the second day that the storm finally cleared, and when Flash arose from a sleep period and went up to the bridge, he found Dr. Zarkov standing alone, his hands clasped behind his back, staring out the forward viewscreens.

Flash joined him, and for a long time neither man said a word. The sight was awesome and somehow hauntingly familiar; it was almost as if there were some kind of ancestral memory built into their genetic makeup. And yet it was not possible.

They were parked in the middle of an absolutely flat, wide, pale blue plain, broken here and there by pockmarks, evidently from explosives or hard-beam laser weapons. The wreckage of what appeared to be a number of spacecraft littered the port, and in the distance to the east and west were a number of very tall towers festooned with huge struts and with girders seemingly running at every angle, with no apparent logic.

For a long time Flash let his mind envision this place as a bustling, active spaceport at the height of the galactic civilization. At a time before the war was finally brought here.

From the holographs Martin had shown them of the people and life of Centrus, he could easily see tens of thousands of gaily dressed men and women coming and going from the various terminal towers, boarding ships of every conceivable shape and nationality bound for planets in a million different star systems. There would have been announcements over some kind of a public hailing system; perhaps music played while passengers waited to catch spaceliners for business or pleasure. Commercial transport vessels would have been unloading a steady stream of goods and products from a million different cultures.

And all of it—every bit of the commerce, the gay life, the sophisticated governmental system, the scientists, the artists and musicians and writers—all of it was centered here on this planet.

Finally Flash allowed himself the pleasure of gazing directly north, at the city itself. Centrus. Jewel of the galaxy, Martin said his creators called it. And the phrase provided an apt description, even now after a devastating war and the passage of twenty thousand years.

The city was white, so vast no outer limits of it could be seen from the ship, and the buildings were shaped like no other buildings Flash had ever seen or could even imagine.

There were towers, so tall and so slender they appeared to be nothing but whispy threads, the tops of which ballooned into semitransparent domes that somehow caught the bright morning sunlight and broke it subtlely into the colors of the rainbow.

There were huge, yet graceful, truncated cones; tall pyramids whose sides were absolutely smooth, and whose peaks were so sharply pointed it was difficult at this distance to determine exactly where the peak ended and the sky began. There were huge shells laying on their sides, the openings all facing inland.

And interlacing the entire city were what appeared to be thin threads running everywhere, at every level, as if millions of huge spiders had spun their webs throughout a vast, white, fairy-tale forest.

The sun had just risen from the east, and overhead in the pale blue sky thousands of stars were still visible, giving a slightly mottled effect to the air. But instead of being disturbing, it lent its own beauty to the scene.

Power. Vast intelligence. Great age. And yet delicacy and sophistication. The city's qualities fleetingly passed through Flash's mind. He finally turned to Zarkov.

"Sandra was right when she guessed that the Citadel computer, as vast as it is, cannot even come close to matching the technology of this place. The Citadel is nothing more than a crude outpost for whoever built this place."

Without taking his eyes from the awesome sight beyond the viewscreens, Zarkov shook his head slowly. "I'm frightened, Flash," he said in a very small voice.

"Nothing showed up on any of the scans?" Flash asked.

"Nothing except the beacon, which is still trans-
mitting from an installation about fifty kilometers
west, up the coast," Zarkov said. He turned slowly
and looked up into Flash's eyes. "But this place is
not dead. It's just switched off."

Flash sucked in his breath and looked again out
the viewscreens. "Like it's waiting for someone.
Waiting for the people to return home."

Zarkov too looked out the viewscreens. "Or
waiting for the rise of new intelligence in the galaxy
to come here and use this place the way it was
meant to be used. To reinhabit the city. Reactivate
its systems. Begin the struggle to build a new galactic civilization. But not us. Not yet. We will be no
more able to understand this city than an early
Earth savage could make sense of New Los Angeles. We don't belong here. It may be a million years
before we do."

"Which means we either return home to Earth
and forget everything we've seen, or we return to
Citadel I and convince the computer to take us
back," Sandra said from the bridge hatch.

Zarkov and Flash turned around as Sandra and
Dale came onto the bridge, and when Dale saw the
view from the forward screens, she uttered a small
cry of delight and rushed forward.

"We will get nothing from this city," Zarkov
said, sighing deeply.

Sandra came across the bridge to look out the
viewscreens. Her expression was impassive. "There
is a museum of technology connected with the
Government Center at the middle of the city. The
computer records did not specify its exact location,
but it's there." She turned to look at Zarkov. "And

it is there, in the museum, where we will find what we have come looking for."

"And what is it we came looking for?" Zarkov asked, unblinking.

"The means to defend ourselves against Citadel II."

"Defend ourselves, or continue the war and perhaps destroy them?"

"Whatever," Sandra said, brushing aside the comment in annoyance. "If we return and bury our heads in the sand, it will be too late for all of us." She pointed out the viewscreens. "And it will be too late for that. We can't give up without trying."

Zarkov once again turned to look at the city, and Flash could see that his old friend was being torn apart with indecision. As a scientist he desperately wanted to go out and find the museum, to investigate the wonders that no doubt they would find. And yet another part of him, the moralistic, sensitive side of him, felt it would be wrong to attempt to tamper with something none of them could hope to adequately understand. It was as if he was afraid of breaking a piece of fragile Proximan crystal that was beautiful to look at, fascinating to contemplate, but that would crumble to dust if touched.

"You saw yourself, Doctor, what the other Citadel is capable of. You saw what it did with our scout ship, despite your best efforts, and despite the last-minute attempt by Martin to get the ship out of the way. What chance do you think we will have against that kind of power? What chance do you think the Earth's Federation will have?" She was bitter now. "None, Doctor. No chance whatsoever. Are you willing to stand by and do nothing to help?"

Despite Dale's suspicions of the woman, and despite the possibility that they all could have been set up to do this by the Citadel computer, Flash had to agree with her. And he could see that Dr. Zarkov was weakening.

"We'll take the hovershuttle into the museum and government center, and nowhere else," Flash said. "We won't touch anything or do anything without your total approval."

Zarkov looked up at Flash as if to say, "You too?" and then he lowered his head. Dale had turned away from the viewscreens, and she reached out and touched her uncle's arm.

"I think Flash is right, uncle," she said. "We've come this far. We can't just turn around and go back. Besides, where would we go? How would we explain this ship if we returned to Earth in it? How would we explain the disappearance of the Goodhope? Or where we had been and what we had done for the past three months?"

They were all silent for several long moments. But finally Zarkov raised his head and nodded slightly, as if he had been defeated and was capitulating. "All right," he said softly. "Let's get it over with and then leave this place until a people who deserve what it has to offer comes along."

The four of them crammed into a tiny hovershuttle, Flash and Zarkov in the front seats and the two women in the back, and took off from the mother ship to hover a moment one thousand meters overhead.

Even at that height the spaceport disappeared in the distance in either direction along the coast. To the south was the sea, and a short distance to the north was the city, which spread inland for as far as they could see.

Before they had left the main ship, Zarkov had run a final series of tests of the atmosphere for everything from dangerous microorganisms to radiation of any kind. The only thing he found was an expectedly high level of ultraviolet radiation from the sun, against which they wore light helmets with sunshields, and gloves. The air quality and temperature, which was a comfortable twenty-five degrees celsius, required that they dress only in their light service coveralls and soft boots.

Flash opened one of the side ports in the hovershuttle, and the outside atmosphere, although somewhat thin, smelled of the sea, wonderfully fresh after their ten-day confinement in the canned air of the space vessel.

He pushed the control forward, and the light craft moved away from the spaceport, over the city, and within a few minutes they were deep inland, the sea lost behind them in the distance. For as far as they could see in any direction, the city gleamed in all its splendor in the morning sun.

The spiderweb threads that connected all the buildings in the city turned out to be narrow walkways less than five meters wide and only a centimeter thick, with no railings or any other visible protective measures to guard against pedestrians falling off. And although there was a light wind blowing from the sea, the thin walkways did not move in the breeze.

Below them, on the ground, were wide boulevards and a regular grid pattern of avenues and streets. No ground vehicles were visible, however, nor did there appear to be any green, living things. Everywhere, though, were elaborately carvèd statues, and fountains, a few of them still spewing water, very much reminiscent of the city back on Citadel I. At least this part of Centrus's culture evidently had been brought to the Citadel by the escaping scientists and technicians.

As they continued inland there seemed to be no end to the vastness of the city, nor was there any sign whatsoever that the place was inhabited now, or had been inhabited for a very long time.

Zarkov had continued scanning the entire electromagnetic communications spectrum with no results, and he switched his monitor console over to radar function, coming up with something almost immediately.

"I'm showing what appears to be a mountain range two hundred kilometers inland," he said. "The city stretches at least that far."

"Do you want more altitude for a positive identification?" Flash asked.

"No," Zarkov answered, and there was a catch in his voice. "But I think I've found the museum."

Sandra snapped forward in the back seat to look over Zarkov's shoulder as he boosted the radar's resolution. "That's it," she said excitedly.

Zarkov looked up from the screen. "Looks like about seventy-five kilometers to the northeast." He glanced back at the screen. "It's on a relative heading of oh-five-oh degrees, but . . ."

Flash turned immediately to the new heading

and then looked over at Zarkov, who was staring out the forward viewing bubble. The old man seemed strangely disturbed. "But what, Doc?" Flash asked.

"If this was anyplace else . . . even the Citadel . . . I'd say what we're approaching is a mountain in the middle of the city. But here . . ." His voice trailed off.

The new course had brought them directly over a very wide boulevard, and in the distance they could see something shimmering. Whatever it was rose much higher than their thousand meters' altitude.

"My God . . .," Dale said softly.

All of them watched with increasing wonder as the thing at the end of the wide avenue grew as they came closer. It was a pyramid, fifteen kilometers on a side at the base, that rose five thousand meters into the pale blue sky. It was white, like every other structure in the vast city, and near its peak were clouds and a small, very faint rainbow.

There were no windows, ports, or other protuberances of any kind along the side of the thing, but at the ground level they could make out wide, dark bands that appeared to be a series of entrances.

The pyramid was surrounded by a shimmering white wall several meters thick and at least a hundred meters tall. A wide gate was open at the end of the boulevard to admit ground vehicles and possibly pedestrians into a courtyard that itself was several kilometers deep. Everything was on a scale that was hard to comprehend even though they were seeing it firsthand. Fountains, statuary, and areas that at one time obviously had contained trees and other living things, were arranged in complex patterns in the courtyard, which was laced with walkways and the boulevard itself that ran straight to the base of the mammoth building. Along the wall to the south and north, other wide avenues led to the wall, and through similar gates into the courtyard.

No one said a word as Flash brought the hovershuttle low over the wall and finally it set down at the avenue's end. A few meters away was a low step, which led to the entrance of the pyramid, and ran, as far as they could tell, the entire fifteen-kilometer length of the building's base.

This close to the structure, they could not make out the fact that it was pyramidal in shape; the wall appeared to be flat, rising out of sight into the sky.

They all climbed out of the hovershuttle after Zarkov had made a quick scan for electromagnetic noise and lifeforms with no results. The building, if it could be called that, appeared to be dead as far as their instruments could determine.

The four of them moved slowly away from the shuttle, mounted the low step, and stopped a couple of meters from the opening which was nothing more than a gap, three meters or so tall, between the building's side and the base.

"There's nothing holding the building up," Dale said softly. She was staring along the side, and the others followed her gaze. For as far as they could see there were no breaks in the gap between the building and its foundation. There were no pillars, no walls, nothing. As far as they could tell, the building, all five thousand meters of it, simply floated three meters above the floor.

"It would take the power output from an entire star to produce a gravity-resist field this huge," Flash said.

Zarkov looked at him and shook his head. "Perhaps they discovered some other principle. Something we have no comprehension of."

Sandra, who had not taken part in the discussion, moved forward, and before anyone could stop her, passed through the opening, a slight shimmer of blue marking her passage. And then she was gone.

"Sandra," Dale cried out and took a step forward, but Flash held her back.

"I'm right here, just inside the building," Sandra's voice came to them. "Can't you see me?"

"No," Flash said. He glanced at Zarkov, who wearily nodded his head.

"Our instruments were wrong; the building lives," he said, and together the three of them stepped through the opening.

Sandra stood a few meters inside the entrance, and she was slowly shaking her head, her hands hanging loosely at her sides.

They were in a vast hall, the far walls and ceiling of which were lost in the distance. The entire space was dimly lit with various colors of light, the source of which was undetectable. But the hall was filled, seemingly to capacity, with a vast array of objects—some lying on low tables, some encased in glass-like cabinets, some hovering a few centimeters from the floor, and some suspended in midair at various heights as high up as they could see. Many of the objects were obviously machines, all of them apparently brand new and in working order.

"The museum," Sandra said in a hushed, almost religious tone when she became aware that the others had joined her.

Zarkov moved forward and shuffled past her down an aisle, the others falling silently in behind him. About a hundred meters or so away from the entrance he stopped at a large, spindly looking machine with four lower struts that all of them recognized as landing pods. It was a very ancient space vessel of some kind. It was obvious. No more than three or four human-size beings could have fit into the small machine that now sat on the floor of the museum, its struts and hull gleaming gold.

"This *is* a museum," Zarkov said after a long moment. He turned to the others. "We're standing now in the midst of a display of very ancient machinery, and unless I miss my guess the displays in one direction, parallel to the entrance, will date from earlier and earlier periods of their history; while the displays in the other direction will become more and more modern."

"But this space vessel is old even by Earth standards," Dale blurted.

"Yes," Zarkov said with a slight smile. "We've got several hundred thousand years' worth of technological development to explore before we come to anything that will help us." He turned to Sandra. "Do you still believe, Miss Debonshire, that we can do any good here?"

But she wasn't looking at him. She was facing the way they had come, and her complexion had turned a deathly white. She tried to say something, but only a strangled gasp came out.

"Sandra?" Dale said, taking a step forward.

Flash had turned to look toward the entrance, and at first he saw nothing. Then a black android appeared through the entry way, and his blood ran cold.

It was a warrior droid, of *Citadel II* design!

CHAPTER 7

Flash, who had taken along one of the ancient .45 automatic weapons from the shuttle craft, pulled it out of his coverall pocket and fired a shot. The bullet ricocheted off the Citadel II warrior droid with no effect on its battle armor, and a moment later four more of the black robots appeared through the entrance.

"They must have been watching this place all along," Zarkov said urgently.

The five warrior droids fanned out from the entryway and headed slowly down the aisles between the displays.

Sandra bolted down the aisle without a word and, dodging between the various displays, headed in a dead run toward the center of the building.

"Sandra!" Dale shouted.

Flash fired again, directly at one of the droid's red eyes, and again the bullet did nothing but ricochet off the machine, neither causing it or the others to slow down nor alter their course.

Flash grabbed Zarkov's arm, and together the two men and Dale headed in the same direction Sandra had gone, working their way as quickly as they could between the displays of various kinds of machinery.

Flash looked back once, after they had gone several hundred meters, and was able to pick out a glint of light reflecting from one of the androids. The droids were apparently keeping a steady pace, just like the ones the computer had designed from extrapolated information for testing back on Citadel I.

A few minutes later, the three of them scooted around a huge machine that looked almost like a plasti steel smelting furnace and stopped. Zarkov was wheezing and coughing, and it was obvious that he would not be able to go much further, at least not at this pace.

Flash peered around the edge of the machine, back the way they had come, but there was no sign of their pursuers. It would not be long, though, he knew, before they would catch up.

"What are we going to do?" Dale said as she too tried to catch her breath.

Zarkov reached out and grabbed Flash's arm. "We must find Miss Debonshire. We can't leave her here. And I think she probably knows more about this place than she told us."

"We have no other choice," Flash said bitterly. "They probably captured or destroyed our hovershuttle, and in all likelihood they got to our shuttle craft back at the spaceport as well." He took the heavy .45 automatic out of his pocket, looked at it a moment, and then laid it in a niche in the machine. "And this won't do us much good either."

Dale stiffled a gasp. "We're stuck here," she said. "But why did Sandra leave us? Where is she going?"

"I don't know," Zarkov said tiredly. "But we've got to try and find her."

"Can you go on?" Flash asked.

Zarkov nodded. "Are they coming yet?"

Flash again looked around the edge of the huge machine, but he could see no sign of the droids. "No," he said. "But they're probably tracking us with heat sensors or some other device. All we can do is put as much distance between us and them as possible until we can figure out what to do."

"Let's go then," Zarkov said, pushing himself away from where he had been leaning against the machine. "As long as we keep ahead of them we'll be all right for a while."

They started off again, both Flash and Dale helping the aging scientist, but at a much slower pace than before.

Sandra had been heading directly toward the center of the building, so far as they could tell, when they lost sight of her, and they continued in that general direction.

Some of the machinery surrounding them looked tantalizingly familiar to Flash, while most of it was totally foreign. Zarkov had been right when he questioned the use of trying to find anything here that would help them. It could take a thousand lifetimes to look through all the displays, and perhaps even then none of them would have any comprehension of what they had seen.

It all seemed so useless. And, for Flash, Earth and his life at New Los Angeles seemed terribly remote and totally irretrievable.

They walked for several hours down the aisles, stopping every now and then for a few minutes to let Zarkov rest. As it got later in the morning the rest periods that Zarkov needed got longer and longer, and they had to stop more frequently.

There had been no sign of the Citadel II warrior droids since their first contact, but Flash was certain they were catching up because of Zarkov's slow pace. Something would have to be done, and soon. There would come a point when Zarkov would be totally unable to continue. And then they would have to wait for the warrior droids to catch up with them.

As they made their way through the displays, Flash had scrutinized every piece of equipment for anything at all that could help them. A weapon. Something to hide in. Or better yet, some kind of a vehicle for transport.

So far, however, he had seen nothing even remotely offering any hope.

They had stopped to rest next to a large glass tube, several meters in diameter and a dozen or so meters high, and after ten minutes Zarkov sighed deeply and looked at Flash. "I'm ready," he said, his voice cracked and barely audible.

"Are you sure?" Flash asked.

Zarkov was about to answer when Dale, who had walked around the side of the glass tube, called to them excitedly.

"Flash . . . uncle . . . come quickly!"

Flash was the first to her side. Beyond the glass

tube he saw that the museum displays ended twenty meters or so down one of the aisles. Across a wide space there was what appeared to be a large door set into a wall that disappeared up into the darkness, then ran left and right for as far as they could see.

Flash went back and helped Zarkov around the glass tube, and the three made their way past the last displays toward the door, which silently slid back into the wall as they got within a couple meters of it.

Inside the door was impenetrable darkness. Flash was about to step toward it when Zarkov stopped him.

"Look," the old man said, and he pointed to a diagram above the doorway.

Flash looked up and instantly recognized the design as a stylized depiction of the Milky Way galaxy. A bright red point glowed near the center of the diagram, evidently indicating this planet.

"Unless I miss my guess," Zarkov said, "this will be the center of the galactic government."

"The assembly hall for delegates?" Dale asked.

"Probably," Zarkov said, looking down from the diagram and trying to peer into the darkness through the doorway. "There'll be probably nothing inside of any use to us," he said after a moment, and he started to turn around when a pinpoint of intense blue light barely missed his head, blasting a small chunk of material from the doorframe.

One of the black droids stood in the aisle next to the glass tube. The instant before it fired a second time, Flash grabbed Zarkov literally off his feet and barreled through the doorway, roughly shoving Dale ahead of him.

As they passed through the opening Flash felt a moment of intense vertigo, as if he had just stopped off a ledge, and the droid behind them fired, the energy from its weapon spreading out as a wide blue circle in the center of the opening, a few centimeters behind them.

"There's some kind of an energy absorption field in here," Flash said.

The droid was joined by the other four Citadel II warrior robots, and together the five of them moved swiftly down the aisle, directly toward the doorway.

Flash pulled Zarkov back, nearly stumbling because the floor slanted sharply downward behind him, away from the door.

"Run for it," Flash shouted to Dale as the first of the droids reached the doorway. But before he could move, the robot was flung backward a half-dozen meters, clattering against the nearest display.

The other four robots stopped and backed up. One of the droids raised its weapon appendage and fired point-blank at the still open doorway, but as before, the only effect was a blue circle at the center of the opening.

The second droid raised its weapon and fired too, only this time the blue dot began to enlarge, the edges becoming cherry red and ragged. The third and fourth machines fired next, enlarging the glowing area even more. The droid that had been flung away from the doorway then struggled upright and quickly joined the others in their attempt to break down the energy field.

"The field won't last very long by the looks of it," Zarkov said, catching his breath somewhat. The man still looked fagged.

"Flash?" Dale shouted from behind them, and they both snapped around.

Dale stood a meter away from them, down a wide ramp that led at a very steep angle deep into the center of a vast, circular auditorium of some kind. Seating for at least five-hundred thousand beings was arranged in tiers around the huge room, many of the seats shaped so oddly that no human being could possibly sit in them. But what immediately caught their attention was what appeared to be a mammoth holographic projection of the Milky Way galaxy suspended beneath a domed ceiling. The projection was alive, the spiral arms of the galaxy rotating slowly, and fanning outward from the center of the depiction were pulsating red dots, tens of thousands of them.

"It's a map," Zarkov said, awed. "It's a map of their civilization."

Beneath the projection, on the floor of the auditorium far below them, was a huge, circular, ebony-colored table, with chairs around it for at least a hundred beings.

Zarkov moved away from Flash and took a couple of steps down the ramp. "From here they must have administered the law for tens of trillions of beings."

Flash turned to look over his shoulder at the doorway. The droids were still working on the force field, and now the blue circle had expanded so that it took up almost a third of the opening.

The edges of the burn pattern glowed a cherry red, and the center was an intense white.

He rushed back to the doorway and frantically searched for some kind of control that would allow him to shut the doors, but there was nothing. Even as he watched, the burn pattern in the force field expanded. They did not have much time.

Zarkov and Dale were still staring at the galactic map, when Flash turned and rushed down to them.

"We've got to get out of here, now! That field won't last much longer!"

Zarkov seemed to come out of his daze, and he looked back toward the doorway. "We could learn so much here," he said. "We could avoid all their mistakes."

"We've got to go, Hans!" Flash shouted. He grabbed Zarkov's arm and as gently as possible pulled the old man with him down the wide ramp, as Dale stumbled ahead of him.

It took them nearly fifteen minutes to reach the bottom, and by then Zarkov was completely worn out; his color was bad, his breath came in ragged gasps, and his face was bathed in an unhealthy-looking perspiration. Dale was not in much better condition.

Above them, up the long ramp, there was still no sign of the warrior droids, so Flash led Zarkov a couple of meters over to the front row of a vast tier of seats and eased the old man down into one.

Instantly a paper-thin, flat plate snapped into place two-thirds of a meter in front of Zarkov at chest height. A moment later the plate came alive with a seating diagram of the entire auditorium, a data screen, and several dozen control areas, each with its own complicated symbol.

"Welcome to Alpha Center," Sandra Debonshire's voice came to them from the control panel in front of Zarkov.

"Sandra . . . where are you? What's happening?" Dale said. She and Flash both stood next to Zarkov.

"I'm seated at the opposite side of the situation table from you."

Flash swiveled around so that he could see across the vast table. For a moment he could not pick her out in the dim light, but then he saw her seated in a tall black chair directly across from them.

"Why'd you run from us . . .?" Dale started to ask, but Flash cut her off.

"Who are you?" he snapped.

"One at a time," the young woman said. There was an intensity to her voice that sounded unnatural.

Flash glanced up the ramp, but the droids apparently had not yet broken through the force field at the door.

"Don't worry about the Citadel II droids," Sandra's voice came to them clearly. "It will be several minutes before they are able to get in here, and by then you will be gone."

"Why were we maneuvered into coming here?" Flash asked, glancing again across the vast table at the young woman.

"That is the fifth question you people have asked me. None of them really has any meaning. If there is time I will explain everything to you, but for the moment you must all listen very closely."

Flash moved away from where Zarkov was seated and started around the table, but Sandra's voice came to him from the control panel.

"Please, Col. Gordon, your life and the lives of Dr. Zarkov and Miss Arden depend upon what I am about to tell you."

Flash stopped and gazed uncertainly toward the young woman. Whoever, or whatever, she was, it was apparent that she bore no similarities to the young woman who two hundred years ago had left Earth orbit aboard an exploration vessel headed for the stars. Biological robot. Pawn of the Citadel I computer. Whatever. They had come this far with her, and now they would have to listen. There was nothing left for them to do.

He moved back to where Zarkov was slumped down in his seat. Dale took Flash's hands in hers.

"I'm glad you decided at least to give me a hearing, Col. Gordon, because despite what you may be thinking at the moment I *am* on your side. I must admit, you and the good doctor and Miss Arden have been maneuvered this far. But it was for your own good. For the good of your own fledgling Federation. You must listen to me with an open mind. And you must help, or else all will be lost."

"I'm listening," Flash said, and he again glanced up the steep ramp, to make sure the droids had not yet burned through the doorway.

"At this moment," Sandra continued, "a vast space vessel is on its way to this planet from Citadel II. For a number of years we have suspected its existence, but now that I've had a chance to use this Center's detection and early-warning devices, as well as its sophisticated long-range scanners, its presence and its purpose have been proven."

"With hyperdrive, why hasn't this supposed vessel already arrived here?" Zarkov asked tiredly. "You speak as if you have known about its journey for some time."

"The ship is on a scientific mission from the other Citadel. It has been for fifty years or so. It is stopping at every planet where any of the original civilization's technology is still intact. Centrus is its second-to-last port of call."

"Second to last?" Flash asked.

"Citadel I will be the last," she said. "Once the ship arrives here it will dismantle this city, and more specifically this Center—chip by chip, disc by disc, field by field. When it is finished it will have gained all the knowledge that is available here. And it will have destroyed this place. The Citadel will be next, at which point no force in this galaxy will be able to offer even the slightest challenge."

"What do you expect us to do?" Zarkov asked.

"Destroy the Mech ship," she said.

"How?" Zarkov asked.

The woman hesitated a moment, and Zarkov repeated his question.

"The droids have broken through the field," she shouted.

Flash looked up as the Citadel II warrior droids started down the ramp, and then he looked back at the young woman across the table. "How do we get out of here?" he shouted.

"Around the situation table, there's a ramp directly behind me. To the right is a portal. Take it.

There are weapons that are effective against such
droids on the other side. Hurry!"

The control board in front of Zarkov vanished,
and the old man was suddenly on his feet in front
of his chair.

Above them the warrior droids were already a
quarter of the way down the ramp, and one of
them fired its weapon, the shot hitting wide of the
mark, blowing the backs off several of the seats.

Flash grabbed Zarkov and together with Dale
they rushed around the huge table toward where
Sandra had remained seated.

Whatever was really happening here, Flash did
not want to be cornered by the warrior droids, at
least not until he had a weapon with which to defend them.

The Citadel II machines were halfway down the
ramp and moving very fast by the time Flash and
the others had made it around the table to Sandra.
Flash broke away from Zarkov and went to pull
Sandra's chair away from the table, but his hands
were stopped in midair at least a meter away from
the seat.

She turned and looked up at him, then shook her
head. "There isn't much time, Col. Gordon. If you
value your life and the lives of Dr. Zarkov and
Miss Arden, you will do as I told you."

Flash stared at the woman for a long time, but
he could fathom nothing in her eyes. It was as if she
was nothing more than a machine herself.

He turned finally, and he and Dale helped
Zarkov to the right of the ramp directly behind
Sandra's chair to a black opening in the wall. They
hesitated a moment, then stepped through the
portal.

The same feeling of vertigo that Flash had felt coming through the doorway at the head of the ramp again assailed his senses. When he looked up he found himself in a small circular room with a low ceiling, several windows, a ramp leading downward from the center of the floor, and several racks arranged like library shelves that held what appeared to be a variety of weapons and other unidentifiable devices.

He quickly helped Zarkov across the room to the ramp. He left the old man there and ran to one of the windows and looked out.

In the distance he could see their shuttle vessel across the pockmarked blue plain. They were back at the spaceport. The portal was a matter transmitter.

Several black vessels, of Citadel II design, were parked around the shuttle. As Flash watched, a blue streak streamed from one of the ships to their shuttle, blasting away a huge section of the hull.

"Flash!" Dale screamed.

He turned around in time to see one of the warrior droids step through the portal. It raised its weapon toward Dale and Zarkov.

Flash leaped to the nearest weapon rack and grabbed at what appeared to be some kind of an assault rifle, but the weapon would not come out of its clamps. He grabbed at another weapon that looked like a laser pistol, but it too was locked in place.

The warrior droid took a step forward away from the portal, its weapon appendage still trained on Zarkov and Dale, as another of the droids appeared in the room.

At that moment Flash grabbed unthinkingly at

another weapon, this one coming free from its
rack. He only had an instant to realize that what he
held in his hand was nothing more than a sword—
an ancient Earth weapon he recognized from one
of Zarkov's books on warfare—when he leaped
forward between Zarkov, Dale, and the droids.

CHAPTER 8

The first droid got off one shot, grazing Flash's side with a searing pain, before he swung the large sword with all of his might, bringing the blade down on the machine's shoulder joint.

In that brief instant the intense pain of his wound was combined with an almost inhuman rage—a blinding, all-consuming urge to kill that he had not felt since his wife had been murdered years ago.

He had no doubt at that moment that they would all die here in this tower outside a city tens of thousands of years old, and halfway across the galaxy from Earth, their home.

But the sword completely severed the droid's firing arm and buried itself to the hilt in its torso. In the next instant Flash had pulled the blade back, swung it over his head with both hands on the broad handle, and brought it down squarely atop the second machine's head, cleaving its left eye, its

neck joint, and its torso nearly to its legs, amid an
intense shower of sparks and spurting fluids.

Flash fell back against one of the weapon racks
and pressed his left hand against his wounded side.

Dale leaped forward with a little cry. "You're
hurt!"

"I'll be all right," he snapped. The rage inside of
him had only slightly subsided. "We've got to get
out of here before the other droids come."

"Where are we?" she said.

"At the spaceport," he said, and he pushed himself away from the rack and staggered back to the
windows in time to see the final destruction of their
shuttle vessel.

A moment later one of the Citadel II spacecraft
lifted slowly off the pad and swung lazily around to
head directly toward the tower.

Flash tried to make his mind work against the
pain that throbbed through his entire body. There
was a ship evidently manned with one or more of
the warrior droids heading their way. And out in
the assembly hall there were three other droids, besides Sandra, who they could not afford to leave
behind. She knew too much about this city and its
functions as well as the Citadel II mechanisms.
They would not stand much of a chance without
her, even with the sword.

He held the weapon up to look at it. Its hilt was
plain, its broad handle obviously designed for a
being with much longer fingers than a human, but
its blade looked like a jewel, as if it was made of
solid ruby or some other deep red precious stone. It
was warm to the touch, and the longer Flash stared
at the blade the more it seemed to shimmer and

waver in front of his eyes, almost as if it was not made of solid substance.

He turned around finally. Zarkov was leaning against one of the equipment racks, barely able to stand. Dale had pulled out another of the large swords, evidently the only kind of weapon that would come free from its clamps, and she was holding it in both hands, peering intently toward the portal that led back to the assembly hall.

"There's a Citadel II vessel coming across the port toward us, and there are three more droids out there," he said, crossing the room to the portal.

"We can't leave Sandra behind," Dale said determinedly.

"I'm going back after her," Flash said. "Stay here with your uncle."

She looked up at him. "Have they destroyed our shuttle?"

Flash nodded, and Dale's lips compressed into a fine line as she tightened the grip on her sword. "Sandra is our only hope. But be careful, Flash."

He took a deep breath, raised his sword, and leaped through the portal, landing in a crouch at the other side below the ramp and a few meters behind the table where Sandra had been seated.

The huge assembly hall was still. The chair Sandra had been seated in was turned over, and beside it on the floor were the scorched, ruined remains of one of the Citadel II warrior droids. But no one or nothing moved in the vast auditorium.

With great care Flash moved forward, away from the portal to the table, from where he gazed around the room toward the entryways far above. Directly overhead the three dimensional map of the galaxy still shimmered brightly in the dim light, but he was absolutely alone here as far as he could tell.

"Sandra!" he shouted, his voice lost in the vastness of the place. "Sandra Debonshire!" he shouted again. He held his breath, straining to listen for a sound, any noise. But he could hear nothing.

She had evidently been captured—or killed—by the warrior droids, and there was little they could do about it now. It was too late for her, and very likely too late for them as well.

He went back to the portal and stepped through it. Dale stood poised at one side of the room away from the ramp, her uncle leaning against the wall behind her. She was white-faced, her entire body rigid. When she saw Flash a look of relief crossed her features, but she urgently motioned him to be silent, and then she pointed upward.

Flash noiselessly crossed the room to her. "Are they here?" he whispered.

"One of the spacecraft docked at the next level above us," she said softly. She looked over Flash's shoulder, back toward the portal. "Where's Sandra?"

"She's gone," Flash said. "She managed to destroy one of the droids, but the other two must have taken her."

"What are we going to do?" she said, looking up into his eyes. She was deeply frightened, but there was a determined expression on her face.

He reached out and touched her cheek with the back of his left hand. "Not give up just yet," he said softly. He turned to Zarkov. The old man was trembling, but it was not from fear, it was from utter exhaustion. "Can you hold on just a little longer, Hans?"

Zarkov managed to nod, but nothing else. A loud thump sounded from above, and Flash looked up at the seamless, white plasti steel ceiling. Then a high-pitched whine began. A thin red line appeared in the ceiling and began moving in a large circle. The droid or droids were cutting through the floor above.

Flash hurried over to the window facing the remains of their shuttle craft, and looked out. The other Citadel II spacecraft were still parked across the port, and looking up he could just see the afterportion of the craft that had docked at this tower.

The red circle in the ceiling was nearly completed, and Flash motioned for Zarkov and Dale to get down as he moved to one side and held his sword at the ready. His side was on fire from the wound and was already starting to stiffen up.

If there were only one or two droids above, they would at least have a chance. If there were more, they'd be lost.

The circle was completed with a snap, and a moment later the circular section of ceiling, which was a couple of meters in diameter, was drawn away. Flash tightened his grip on the weapon.

For several long seconds nothing happened. There was no movement from above, and Flash was about to edge closer when a wide beam of yellow light, as wide around as the hole, shot down from the ceiling with a soft hum, and two droids descended within the beam as if they were climbing down the rungs of a circular stairway.

Flash leaped forward and swung the sword with all of his might directly at the nearest droid, but when the blade encountered the light beam, it stopped as if he had smashed into an armor plate. A stunning burst of pain coursed through his body from the wound in his side.

The light beam went out, and with blinding speed both droids raised their weapons and fired at Flash, green threads wrapping themselves around his body, completely immobilizing him.

As he was falling he saw Dale leap to the warrior robots from behind and slash with her sword, cutting both of the machines nearly in two. Instantly the tangled web holding Flash released itself, and he was able to get shakily back to his feet.

Dale was in his arms, sobbing and shaking uncontrollably. "I thought they had killed you . . . I didn't know what to do . . . I thought you were dead . . . ," she stuttered.

Flash looked up at the opening in the ceiling, but there was no sign of any more of the droids. "We've got to get out of here," he said.

"I don't think I can," Dale sobbed.

"We must!" Flash snapped.

Zarkov had somehow managed to push himself away from the wall, and he stumbled across the room to them. His color was somewhat better than before. "If their ship is anything like the extrapolated designs we've seen back at Citadel I, we'll be able to handle it."

"Exactly," Flash said. "But we're running out of time. It won't be long before another of the ships will be here to investigate." He started back to the hole in the ceiling, but Zarkov stopped him.

"The key may be here after all, if Sandra was telling the truth about the Citadel II's Mech ship, as she called it. It cannot be allowed to get this far and destroy this place. It cannot!"

"Then it's up to us to stop it. Somehow," Flash said. He went across the room to stand directly beneath the hole. The ceiling was something less than three meters high, but with the gravity on this planet somewhat less than Earth normal, getting up would be no real problem.

He crouched down and, still holding his sword at the ready, leaped up, catching the edge of the hole and pulling himself into the room above. Again the pain slammed at him from his side.

A hatchway to the right was open, revealing the interior of the Citadel II ship bathed in dim red light. Other hatches around the circular room were closed, and toward one side was a wide area of pale blue material set in the floor.

In all probability this place had been used as one of the passenger terminals for arriving and departing space vessels. The room below was the armory for spaceport security, necessarily sealed off from normal passenger areas.

"Are you all right?" Dale called up to him.

He leaned over the hole in the floor and looked down at Dale, who stood looking up. "The ship is here and apparently deserted. Can you boost your uncle up high enough for me to grab him?"

"I'll try," she said, and she laid her sword down and led Zarkov to a position directly beneath the opening. Flash lay on his stomach and extended his arms as far down into the room as he possibly could.

Dale cupped her hands together, interlocking her fingers, and the aging scientist somehow managed to step up, one hand holding onto her head, the other reaching upward. His entire body was shaking as Flash strained every muscle trying to reach the old man, the pain from his wound coming at him in waves.

For a moment it looked as if Dale could not hold the old man's weight, nor could Zarkov raise his hand any further without losing his balance, but finally Flash caught ahold of the scientist's right wrist, and then his left.

An instant later Flash had pulled the panting Zarkov up into the room, and then he reached back down for Dale, who leaped easily into his grip with her sword in the other hand, and he drew her up into the room as well.

He and Dale helped Zarkov through the hatch into the Citadel II vessel, which was little more than a bridge with a half-dozen unpadded acceleration couches and a relatively uncomplicated control console that was attached to the front of what apparently was a sealed drive compartment.

They strapped Zarkov into one of the couches and then climbed into the pair of seats that were directly in front of the main control board.

Flash studied the controls, data screens, and other mechanisms for several long moments, identifying most of them but not all. One set of controls in particular bothered him; they were bordered with a red outline, and a series of red stars as symbols marked each unit.

"The red stars," Flash said over his shoulder to Zarkov, "what do they control?"

"Weaponry, I think," Zarkov croaked.

"Can you fly it?" Dale asked.

Flash took a deep breath and managed a slight smile. "I'm sure going to try," he said, and he reached out and punched the button for the airlock. The hatch behind them closed smoothly, and a moment later the control board came alive with flashing lights of various colors and intensities. Terminal screens across which streams of data and diagrams flowed appeared above the controls. The forward viewscreens showed the terminal hatch on the tower closed and ringed in green.

A communications channel opened, and a series of high-pitched squeals and squeaks blasted from a sound inducer until Flash located the cut-off control and switched the sound off.

"Someone is trying to find out what's going on over here," Flash said. "We're going to have company any moment now."

He hit the drive units, gravity-resist control, and hull defense screens, and slowly eased the compact space vessel away from the terminal tower, turning smoothly so that his forward viewplates were facing the other Citadel II ships.

With one hand he flipped open the weapons-arming switch, and with the other hit the acceleration control, and the ship slammed forward, the acceleration pressing them hard against the acceleration couches despite the gravity-resist override, which was common on all fighting vessels, even of Citadel design.

"Hold on," Flash shouted, and as he swooped in for an attack run, the other Citadel II ships all started to rise.

At the last moment he hit the fire control buttons, and what appeared to be hard-beam laser lances shot out from the bow, automatically seeking their targets.

The fight was over in a matter of seconds. Nothing remained of the four Citadel II vessels other than blackened wreckage that littered the field near the destroyed remnants of their own shuttle vessel.

Flash banked low to the north and set a course back toward the government center and museum at the middle of the city before he glanced over at Dale. She was staring at him with an odd expression in her eyes.

"What's the matter?" he asked, the adrenalin, which had pumped through his body, fading away, leaving him weary, slightly nauseous, and in deep pain from his wound.

"Sandra could have been aboard one of those vessels," she said.

"I know," he answered tiredly, and he turned to stare at the city below them through the forward viewscreens. "I know."

For several minutes they said nothing more to each other, nor did Zarkov, who had lain his head back and closed his eyes, say anything.

He had fought to win—it was as simple as that, he told himself. Under the circumstances they were in, he could have taken no other action and still succeeded. Thinking of the danger to Sandra simply had not been possible.

He closed his eyes momentarily against the pain, not only from his side, but from his mind, which kept going back to his wife's mutilated body and then to the terrible destruction he had wrecked on the men who were responsible for her death. He had been like a man possessed, or rather like a man for whom there was no such concept as control or moderation. Then too he had fought to win.

Or had he fought so fiercely because he wanted revenge? Was he still seeking revenge?

He opened his eyes to glance again at Dale, who was staring intently out the viewscreens. In silence they came over the wall outside the mammoth government center pyramid. They touched down lightly next to the twisted wreckage of their hovershuttle and the still-smoking, charred remains of a Citadel II vessel.

Zarkov had opened his eyes and he leaned forward in his acceleration couch, a grim expression at the corners of his mouth. "Evidently our Miss Debonshire was not taken captive or killed after all," he said.

Once he had the engines shut down, Flash unbuckled himself from his seat and twisted around to look at Zarkov. "It's also evident that she knows considerably more about defending herself than we suspected."

"But where is she then?" Dale asked.

"We're going to try to find that out right now," Flash said. He reached back and hit the control for the main hatch, shoved his acceleration couch back on its gimbals, and jumped down to the deck.

Zarkov started to struggle out of his harness, but Flash gently pushed him back. "Wait here and rest. You can keep an eye on the communicator to make sure no more visitors drop in on us unexpectedly."

Zarkov slumped back, in no condition to argue. "Be careful," he said.

Dale had jumped down from her couch, and she looked sharply at her uncle. "There's none of the Citadel II droids left, are there?"

"I mean, be careful of Miss Debonshire."

"I . . . ," Dale said, but she choked it off. "We have to find her."

"I agree, Dale, but be careful nonetheless."

"Yes, uncle," she said dutifully, and she gently squeezed his arm. Together she and Flash left the ship and headed across the courtyard to the step that led back into the vast building.

Almost immediately both of them stopped in their tracks, and Flash raised the sword he still carried. An uneasiness suddenly was beginning to build up inside of him; at first it was nothing more than a vague feeling that someone or something was behind him, and he swiveled around. But nothing was there except the ship they had just left.

"Do you feel it?" he asked after a long moment.

Dale nodded. "It's like . . . like . . ."

"Like when we first came into the city on Citadel I. The same sounds."

They both looked up, toward the west, as a rainbow seemed to shoot over the sun, accompanied by a deep, barely detectable rumbling.

Every muscle in Flash's body went tense, his skin prickled, his stomach flopped over, and he stepped back a pace toward their ship, pulling Dale with him.

Rapidly the area beneath the vivid, unearthly rainbow began to fill with a swirling, almost blinding pattern of colors and flashes of light, all accompanied by tones, almost musical now, but still soft.

Flash felt drawn forward, and yet some rational

portion of his mind willed him to move back to the safety of the ship.

Soft lights began illuminating the side of the huge pyramid that towered overhead, merging and shifting in a kaleidoscopic display of patterns that moved faster and faster.

The thing in the western sky continued to grow, blotting out the sun and the stars that had been visible, and the patterns of colors shifted still faster, the musical tones matching the speed and intensity of the display.

Dale raised her hands to her head and began to scream and shudder uncontrollably. With the last vestiges of his control Flash grabbed her and stumbled back to the ship, heaving his body up the wide ramp and pulling Dale after him. Visions of his wife, of sailing on the Earth's South Pacific, of flying his own ship, and of playing Tri-V matches all raced through his mind in blinding speed and reality; yet amid his confusion he understood that the ship's hatch was closing and that the vessel was accelerating away from the government center. Then he lost conscious control of his body as even more blinding patterns of light became his entire world.

CHAPTER 9

Someone was calling his name over and over again, and Flash Gordon looked up through a long, dim tunnel into Dr. Zarkov's kindly but worried face. He watched the old man's lips move, and a moment later, like an unsynchronized holographic projection, the sound came to his ears.

"Flash," the old man said again. "Can you hear me?"

Gradually the tunnel faded as Flash regained his peripheral vision, and he became aware that he was lying on his back on the deck of the Citadel II war ship, the one they had stolen from the terminal tower on Centrus.

Other things came back to him as well—painful memories of the thing in the sky. And then it was all clear to him. He sat up with a start.

"Thank God," Zarkov said, and he helped Flash get unsteadily to his feet.

"What happened, Doc?" Flash asked. He ran his

fingers through his hair. The pain from the wound in his side was still sharp, but added to it now was a splitting headache; or more accurately, it felt to him like the back of his head was about ready to blow off.

"Here inside the ship I was apparently insulated from the effects of whatever happened outside. So, I could close the hatch once you and Dale had managed to crawl inside, and then get us out of there."

Flash looked around, spotting Dale strapped into an acceleration couch.

"I managed to get her up onto a couch," Zarkov said. "But not you."

Flash went forward to her and felt for a pulse from her carotid artery in her neck. It was strong and regular, as was her breathing, but she was unconscious.

Zarkov joined him. "She's been like that ever since you managed to drag her aboard."

Flash turned to him. "How long have we been out?"

"An hour or so," Zarkov shrugged.

Flash looked forward to the control console and viewscreens, but there were no indications that anything was working, and yet he could feel the thrum of the ship's engines and systems through the deck.

"What's happening with the ship? Where are we?"

Zarkov shook his head. "I don't know for sure, but I can guess."

Flash went all the way forward to study the apparently dead control board. Not even the drive engine monitors showed any readings. They were completely blind. He reached out and hit the viewscreen controls, with no response whatsoever.

After a moment he turned to peer back at Zarkov, who looked ghostly in the dim red light. "What happened? How long have we been running dead like this?"

"Since we achieved orbit," Zarkov said. He sighed deeply. "We were less than a thousand kilometers out, and I was getting ready to stabilize our position so that I could see to you and Dale, when everything went dead, including the forward screens." He shook his head. "At first I thought it was some kind of a sequencing malfunction, but the engine continued to accelerate us—you can feel it—and nothing I could do seemed to have any effect."

"And it's been like that ever since?" Flash asked.

Zarkov nodded. "I think we're on our way to the Mech ship Miss Debonshire was so worried about."

Flash went back to the hatch area and searched the deck and around the rear acceleration couches in the dim light.

Zarkov called back to him, "You won't find the swords, Flash. You and Dale dropped them outside the ship."

Flash came back to him. "No other weapons aboard?" he asked. "Nothing we can use?"

"Nothing," Zarkov said. "Nor is there any food or water, or any way off this bridge. All we have is breathable atmosphere. Nothing more."

Flash studied the control console for a long moment. "Have you looked inside? If we're on external control, perhaps there's an override circuit somewhere that we can activate."

"I've tried everything," the old man said tiredly. He eased his body into an acceleration couch, lay back, and closed his eyes. "Everything aboard this ship is either molecularly sealed or makes no sense whatsoever. And even if we had a debonding tool, I have a feeling I wouldn't be able to do much good. I couldn't find any seams, or even any bonding points."

Zarkov looked extremely tired, but the expression on his face was peaceful, if resigned. There was little they could do except wait for whatever was in store for them.

Flash went back to where Dale was strapped into one of the acceleration couches. She was still unconscious, but it looked as if she was sleeping peacefully. Her pulse was still strong, her breathing deep and regular, and her temperature felt normal. How long she would be out, however, there was no way of telling.

He stared at her for a long moment. She had a pretty face, much like his wife's. For a brief, disturbing moment he could not visualize his wife at all, and something stirred deep inside him for this woman lying helpless and so dependent upon him and her uncle. Then the feeling passed.

As he started to turn around the ship gave a violent lurch, and an instant later the control console came alive, the forward viewscreens shimmering into life as well.

When he regained his balance, Flash rushed forward and quickly climbed into the acceleration couch. Zarkov had strapped himself down, and he powered his seat forward into the control position. A moment later Flash's seat was locked into place as well.

An apparently very large vessel of some kind had just come out of hyperdrive, because a huge warp-exit corona lay across their bow in the distance, a bright rose color against the multitude of white stars.

Zarkov was working with the detection and scanning equipment as Flash regained directional control of their ship.

"It's of Citadel II design," Zarkov snapped. "I'm sure it's the Mech ship. They've lost temporary control of us in the jump, but it won't last."

Flash flipped the weaponry arming switch, and once the attack scanner was locked into place, he hit the fire control buttons on all four laser-lance banks.

The hard-beam laser weapons pulsed in sequence, the ultrahigh energy bundles stabbing across space toward their target. One went wide of the mark. Two of the beams encountered defense shields and were deflected, but the fourth hit its mark with a blinding white explosion.

"Hit amidships," Zarkov called from his scanner.

Instantly Flash slammed the ship into a tight clearing turn as he cranked full gravity-resist power, but even then they were thrown violently to one side.

He held the ship over for a full two seconds and then slammed the reaction engines hard in the opposite direction for another firing run. A tractor beam slammed into the side of their hull, held for a sickening moment, but then slipped off.

The Mech ship's image slid into the attack scanner, and once again Flash loosed all four banks of laser lances as he cranked up maximum real-space power directly toward the huge ship.

This time two of the high-energy pulses hit their mark, again amidships, in blinding explosions.

Flash started to heel their vessel over for a second clearing turn preparatory to a third attack run, when a tractor beam slammed hard on the hull and held, threatening to crush their ship. Their directional gyros and gravity-resist generators whined up the scale and finally blew their power and impeller units. They stopped dead in space without controls.

A moment later their laser-lance weapon banks overloaded and blew, destroying the attack pods and scanner detectors projecting from either side of the hull beneath and slightly behind the bridge.

Zarkov, who had been hunched over the scanner hood, sat up and shook his head. "We're blind," he said, "except for the forward viewscreens."

Zarkov reached up to swing the astrogation module toward him, when the control board went dead. The reaction engines ceased functioning, the bridge illumination died, and the life-support ventilators slowly wound down, leaving them totally dead except for the still-functioning forward viewscreens.

The tractor beam that held them whined up the scale, and they began moving forward, drawn toward the distant Mech ship that was still furiously burning amidships. Flash moved his acceleration couch back on its gimbals, undid his harnesses, and went back to check on Dale.

She was just coming around, and for a moment she apparently did not recognize Flash in the dim illumination coming from the forward screens. She shrank back in her couch, holding her hands out as if she was trying to ward him away.

"No more," she whimpered. "Please ... no more."

"It's all right," Flash said, taking her hands in his. "It's over now. Everything is all right."

Her eyes seemed to focus and unfocus. "Flash?" she whimpered.

She was still suffering from the after effects of the thing in the sky back on Centrus. There was a haunted look on her face, as if she was trying without success to forget a horrible dream.

Slowly, however, she became aware of the fact that the ship was dark and that the engines were not functioning. She sat forward, clawing at her harnesses as she strained to look past Flash at the forward screens.

"Where are we?" she demanded sharply. She looked up at him. "What's happening to us? Why is it dark in here?"

Flash turned to look forward, and in that instant Dale caught a glimpse of the burning ship dead ahead, and she sucked in her breath.

"It's the Mech ship," she said. She managed to undo her harnesses, and she got shakily out of the acceleration couch. "It's burning. What happened? What in God's name is happening, Flash?"

Without waiting for Flash to answer, she pushed past him and went forward behind Zarkov's acceleration couch. She stared up at the screen. They

were very close to the aft section of the Mech ship
now, and in the distance to port the huge vessel was
burning. Even as they watched, explosions
wracked the ship.

Directly ahead of them was what appeared to be
a wide landing bay, ringed in white lights. The
main hatch was open, the deck's atmospheric integrity evidently secured with some kind of an energy
field.

They were being drawn directly toward the opening, and within the well-lit interior they could see
several parked vessels of the same design as the one
they were on, but the landing bay seemed to be
deserted of droids.

The ship loomed larger, and then they were beneath an overhang. Finally they came through the
landing bay opening and touched down smoothly.

For several long seconds they all stared out the
screens into the huge deck area. High up on the
rear bulkhead were several long rows of windows
or observation ports. Smoke was pouring from a
series of ventilators above the windows, and Flash
suddenly had a vision of them and the Mech ship's
being destroyed together.

"We're getting out of here," he shouted, and he
went aft to the airlock and hit the cycle button. The
hatch slid open, and instantly their ship was filled
with the acrid smell of smoke, accompanied by a
sharp drop in atmospheric pressure.

Zarkov had struggled out of his harnesses, and
Dale helped him aft to the open hatch.

Directly across the landing bay from them,
about fifty meters distant, was one of the war ships,
its hatch open.

"I'll go first," Flash said. "If it's clear I'll motion for you."

"We're sticking together," Dale shouted, and she grabbed for him.

"No," Flash snapped. He pulled away and leaped out the hatch onto the hangar deck. Zarkov called out to him as he landed.

Two steps away from the ship, Flash half-turned to find out what Zarkov had tried to tell him, when a warrior droid came through a doorway on the rear bulkhead, raised its weapon, and fired. From the angle at which he stood, Flash just saw the motion from the corner of his eye. He managed to leap sideways quickly enough so that the blue beam barely missed him, blowing away a section of the deck a few centimeters from his feet.

In the next instant, he dove to the right as the droid fired another shot, the heat of the near-miss warm on his back. Then he was running and dodging, left and right across the landing bay toward the other ship, the wound in his side from his earlier encounter with the warrior droids still sharply painful.

Halfway there a tremendous explosion rocked the entire Mech ship, sending him sprawling, half-dazed, to the deck. The ship was shuddering unnaturally, and as Flash got to his hands and knees another explosion knocked him flat on his back. The windows high on the rear bulkhead blew outward, and flames roared from the openings.

The ship was breaking up, and unless they got aboard one of the war vessels and made it clear they would die with it.

Smoke was thick in the landing bay and the air

nearly impossible to breathe, as Flash managed to get shakily to his feet in time to see Dale struggling toward him with Zarkov.

The deck was heaving beneath his feet, and the droid that had fired at him was buried beneath a pile of debris from the partially collapsed rear bulkhead.

He struggled back across the vibrating deck, and when he reached them, grabbed the old man and headed again toward the warship, Dale following behind.

A few meters away from the open hatch of the other ship Zarkov was overcome by smoke and collapsed. Flash had to literally drag him the rest of the way, up the ramp and into the ship.

He unceremoniously dumped the old man into one of the acceleration couches, then went back to the open hatch where he hit the cycle button. The airlock door closed.

"Flash!" Dale cried, and he spun around and rushed forward to where she stood motionless by the control console.

"What's wrong . . . ?" Flash started to say, but the words died on his lips.

From the outside, this ship looked exactly like the one they had just left, and almost exactly like the Citadel I extrapolated designs. But here at the control board, everything was different. Nothing was where it should be. There were no overhead communications or astrogation modules. There didn't seem to be any forward screens. And none of the few controls on the starkly simplistic board were labeled, or even set in any recognizable patterns.

Another massive explosion rocked the huge Mech ship, and the deck lurched sharply to starboard.

They had run out of time.

"Strap yourself in," Flash shouted, and he climbed into the acceleration couch, secured his harnesses, and fumbled for the seat control, one thing that was where it was supposed to be. His couch moved forward and locked into place.

The control board came alive, and the air a meter in front of him shimmered into life, presenting a panoramic, 360-degree image of the landing bay.

He saw that a half-dozen warrior droids had come through the hole in the rear bulkhead of the landing bay and were rapidly setting up what appeared to be a large assault cannon.

"Hang on," Flash shouted, and he reached out, hesitated a moment, his fingers hovering over the control board, and then he hit a button. Nothing happened. He stabbed at another button with no response, then a third and a fourth, as the droids finished setting up the cannon and stepped aside.

"Flash!" Dale screamed, but at that instant a deep blue beam shot from the end of the weapon, and Flash felt a rushing sensation that stunned his senses.

He was only dimly aware that the control board had come alive with rapidly shifting patterns of lights. Then everything went stark white.

CHAPTER 10

The Centrus port beacon chimed on the Citadel II warship as Flash became aware by degrees that they were somehow alive, that they were no longer aboard the Mech ship's landing bay, and finally that they were descending back to the spaceport from a height of less than two thousand meters.

Dale, strapped into the acceleration couch next to his, was just beginning to come around, as was Zarkov, who was seated in one of the couches near the airlock.

The ship's ventilators had cleared the air of smoke, but there was still the sharp, metallic taste of it at the back of Flash's throat.

They were coming in for a landing near the wreckage of the shuttle craft that had brought them here from Citadel I, which was ringed by debris from the warships Flash had destroyed.

Flash found that he was almost totally incapable of action, and at that moment their entire incredible odyssey came crashing down upon him, its weight almost physical. Every step they had taken, everything they had seen, every place they had been, everything that had been done to them, seemed to push them farther and farther away from Earth.

And· yet it all seemed unreal to him now. It seemed as if it had been a dream, and that soon he would awaken in his bed back in New Los Angeles.

"Where are we, Flash?" Zarkov called from aft. "It feels like we're coming in for a landing."

Flash turned to look over the back of his seat. Zarkov was leaning forward, trying to see the forward view area. "We're coming into Centrus's spaceport. But I don't know how."

"How long has it been?"

"Since we were at the Mech ship?" Flash asked. Zarkov nodded.

"A couple of minutes, I think."

Zarkov sat back and sighed deeply. "I know how we got here," he said. "We've got one of their matter-energy ships."

"How'd we get off the Mech ship? None of the controls responded."

"The drive unit was probably keyed to the defensive shields. The board should respond now that we're away from the Mech ship."

Flash turned back to study the control panel across which streams of lights pulsed in regular order. The closer they came to touchdown, the slower the pulsing became.

He reached out to touch one of the controls, but then pulled his hand back. The ship evidently was riding the Centrus beacon in, and once they had touched down there would be plenty of time to figure out the board.

The ship's landing struts locked into place automatically, and a few moments later they touched down. The bridge lights changed from a dim, battle red to a soft white, and the position gyros whined down as did the subspace reaction engines.

Dale was lying back in her acceleration couch, staring expressionlessly out the forward view area. Flash swiveled in his seat to look at her, and he reached out to touch her arm.

She turned slowly to look at him. There was a strange detachment in her eyes.

"Dale?" Flash said, tightening the pressure on her arm.

She looked down at his hand, and then back up. "We're back on Centrus," she said softly, no emotion in her voice. It was almost as if she were an automaton.

Flash powered his acceleration couch back to the locked position, released his harnesses, and jumped down to the deck.

The couches were set fairly high up from the deck, and he had to reach up to release Dale's retaining straps. She tried to push his hands away idly, almost as if she were brushing away an insect in her sleep.

"Leave me alone," she said sleepily. "I don't want any more."

"Dale, listen to me," Flash said, releasing the last of her harnesses. She slumped slightly forward.

"I want to go home," she half-mumbled, half-cried.

"Listen to me, Dale," he said, reaching up and

taking her shoulders. "We all want to go home. But first we've got to finish what we came here for."

She looked at him. "The Mech ship has been destroyed. Hasn't it?"

Flash nodded. "And now we must find Sandra."

"No. She's dead. We're alone here."

"I don't think so. We saw the wreckage of the warship by the government center. I think she did that. She's still here on Centrus."

"It's none of our business, Flash. Let's go home. We can hide this ship when we get back. We don't have to tell them anything." Dale's eyes were shining.

"There is still the problem of Citadel II. They won't quit with just one Mech ship. Sooner or later they'll come back here. Then they'll destroy Citadel I. Our Federation wouldn't stand a chance."

"There's nothing we can do about it!" she shouted. "We're like children against them! We can't fight them!"

"We can and we must," Flash snapped. "We've already destroyed four of their warships. We've destroyed their Mech ship. And now we've got one of their matter-energy drives. We can fight them, and we must. Before it's too late."

"I can't," she said, turning her head away.

Zarkov had come forward, and he took one of Dale's hands in his. "Flash is right, sweetheart, we need your help."

She turned back. "Uncle?" she said in a small voice.

"Miss Debonshire is a machine, or at least she's

been programmed by a machine for a specific function."

Dale said nothing, and Zarkov glanced up at Flash before he continued.

"You are a computer psychologist, and a very good one. We need your help in this. What did Miss Debonshire do after we left her? If she is machine-programmed, where would she be at this moment? What would she be doing? We must find her."

A wild look came into Dale's eyes, and she glanced out the forward view area still shimmering above the control panel. "What about the thing in the sky?" she asked in a shaky voice.

Zarkov said nothing, and Dale turned back to him and Flash.

"What about it, uncle?" she said, raising her voice. "Flash?"

Flash shook his head. Everything else she had been able to handle. The fighting, the loneliness, the hunger. But not that . . . whatever it was they had seen in the sky here and back on Citadel I. "I don't know, Dale. Even Martin said he didn't know."

"We have no defense against it. When it happens we're nearly helpless. Twice it has gotten us. What happens the third time?"

"Maybe there is an answer at the museum," Zarkov said tiredly. He too glanced out the forward view area.

"Or maybe there is no answer, uncle. Maybe it's something we'll never understand. Maybe it's the basic power source for this city. Like electricity for our machines. If we don't understand its basic principles, how can we hope to understand their machines?"

"She's right, of course," Zarkov said tiredly.

"Yes," Flash said. He too was tired and hungry. They had not eaten now in what seemed like months. "Nevertheless, we can't give up without trying."

"She'll be looking for weapons and waiting for us," Dale said softly.

Flash and Zarkov both turned to look at her. She was staring at the city across the spaceport from them.

"Back at the museum?" Flash asked.

Dale looked at him and nodded. "There'll be a message of some sort for us at the government center. If we were successful in destroying the Mech ship, we would return here, and the message would tell us what to do next. If we were not successful, the message wouldn't matter. Either way she will be searching for weapons." She paused for a moment. "Either way there could be food and drink waiting for us as well."

"We could just stay here until she comes for us . . . ," Flash started to say, but Dale cut him off.

"She's probably aware we have returned, but she won't come here. If we sit and wait we would be of no use to her. We must initiate the action."

Flash turned to study the ship's control panel. "It's going to take a while to figure this out," he said.

"We don't have to," Zarkov said, and he nodded toward the view area. "We can walk across the field to the terminal tower and take the portal back to the government center."

"Are you up to it, Doc?" Flash asked.

"If we remain here, we starve," the old man said.

They were silent for a long moment until Flash reached out to help Dale down from her acceleration couch, and then they all went aft. Zarkov opened the airlock.

The outside atmosphere smelled sweet and fresh, and Flash took a deep breath, letting it out slowly.

"How's your side?" Dale asked him before they left the warship. Now that a decision had been made, she seemed to be more her old self.

He touched her cheek with his fingertips. "I'll live," he said.

She smiled up at him. "I hope so," she said softly, and together the three of them left the ship and headed across the field toward the terminal tower they had entered through the portal from the government center.

The sun was bright, the breeze gentle, and the day warm. It seemed to Flash almost as if they were taking a leisurely stroll, not heading on a search for weapons that would help them destroy a machine-based civilization bent on annihilating them.

The tower was at least three kilometers across the field, but because of the pleasant weather and the less than Earth-normal gravity, Zarkov seemed to hold up well.

None of them said a thing during the walk, which took them the better part of forty-five minutes, and Flash let his thoughts drift. This planet, and the space nearby where the Mech ship had come out of hyperdrive, had been the scene of the first real battle in this continuation of an eighty-thousand-year war. Where would the next battle be held? What force or forces would be used? And how high would the casualties be?

But what was most frightening to him, was the thought that Earth itself could become the scene of a battle. A short-lived battle to be sure, but one in which the number of casualties would be appalling.

It was near noon by the time they reached the base of the tower, which rose several hundred meters above the level of the field. Docking bays ringed the structure every twenty meters or so upward, but at ground level there were a series of wide entrances. All of them were open.

"How far up is the weapons room where the portal is located?" Zarkov asked. He was winded.

"It's just below the first docking bays," Flash said, looking up. "If we can get to it. The place may be sealed off."

Dale looked across the field toward the city in the distance. "I don't relish the idea of trying to hike a couple of hundred kilometers through the city," she said.

"Neither do I," Flash said.

The three of them mounted a single low step, slowly crossed what appeared to be a wide pedestrian mall, and entered the tower.

They found themselves in a large, circular room with a central ramp that led upward. The place looked like the terminal center on any Federation spaceport, with ticket counters along the walls and data screens above them upon which flight information would be flashed. Ten meters above the main level was a broad concourse where various shops were located.

Even from here they could see that the shop windows were bare, and more than anything else they had seen on this planet, this place had the definite look and feel of great age and desertion.

They trudged across the main level and headed up the ramp to the concourse level. This place, like the city inland, had withstood the ravages of time for many thousands of years. And during the time this place had been occupied, how many millions of feet had trod this ramp? How many voices had been raised in greetings or in good-byes?

Flash stopped at the concourse level and looked across one of the spidery bridges at the now-empty shops. Trinkets and curios from a million cultures had been bought and sold here. The feeling that they were intruders, that they were walking over an ancient grave, was strong within Flash, and he turned up the ramp and continued upward, Dale and Zarkov directly behind him.

Halfway up the ramp to the next level, Flash looked up. He could see a round hole cut in the ceiling of the room above, and he hurried up.

The wreckage of the two droids he had done battle with still lay in a heap near the portal entrance, and the two droids Dale had destroyed were still beneath the hole. As far as he could tell nothing had been disturbed.

A moment later Dale and Zarkov joined him as he crossed the room to one of the weapons racks and selected a short sword with a ruby blade. The weapon came easily free of its clamps, and he hefted it a moment before he stuck it in his belt.

It seemed a little melodramatic to be carrying the ancient blade, but so far it had been the only effective weapon against the warrior robots.

Flash was the first through the portal back into the government center, Dale and Zarkov stepping through immediately after him.

They paused in the lee of the ramp that led upward toward one of the entrances to the main assembly hall for several long seconds trying to detect any motion, trying to determine if they were alone here.

Flash took a step forward, closer to the large table. "Sandra!" he shouted, his voice sounding puny and insignificant in the vast space.

An instant later his eyes strayed to the chair in which she had been seated, the chair that he had found tipped over before, next to a downed robot. His heart skipped a beat.

The droid was gone, and the chair had been turned upright and pushed nearly all the way back to the table.

He quickly drew his sword, motioned for Dale and her uncle to hold back, and he moved forward on the balls of his feet, ready to spring in any direction he had to.

But there was no challenge. No movement. No attack. And no sign whatsoever that there had been a struggle here earlier.

He stopped just behind the chair Sandra had been seated in and looked up at the empty seats around the vast auditorium, and again he could envision this place teeming with activity. Tens of thousands of intelligent beings all focusing in on the chosen hundred seated here at this table. All hammering out the rules and laws governing trillions of beings spread across a vast galaxy.

The power emanating from this place was awesome, even now, thousands of years after it had been deserted.

Zarkov and Dale came up behind him, and he turned to them as he stuffed the sword back into his belt. "She was here after the attack," he said. "There was a droid lying on the floor and her chair was tipped over."

Without a word Dale brushed past him and pulled Sandra's chair away from the table, then reached forward. "Here it is," she said, straightening up and turning back. She held a small black disc up for them to see. "This is probably a message disc of some sort."

Flash took the disc from her, examined it a moment, then handed it to Zarkov. "What do you make of it, Doc?"

Zarkov turned the thing over in his hands, then held it up to the dim light coming from the galactic map overhead. "Impossible to tell just by looking at it," he said. "But if it is some kind of a message disc, there has to be an information retrieval unit here somewhere."

Flash stepped around to the front of Sandra's chair and ran the fingertips of his right hand over the smooth, highly polished ebony tabletop. There were no lines, no seams, no indications whatsoever of any disc player equipment, or anything else for that matter.

But then, he thought, there had been no indication of any kind of control panel before they had sat Zarkov down in one of the auditorium seats.

He pulled the large chair closer to the table and sat down. Instantly a section of the tabletop about a half-meter square rose up at a slight angle in front of him, almost like a drafting screen.

The section was lit up with a series of controls and data screens similar to the board in front of the auditorium seat Zarkov had sat in earlier. Near the bottom of the panel was a narrow slot, obviously meant for the message disc.

"Here it is," he said, looking up. He took the message disc from Zarkov, and after just a moment's hesitation he dropped it into the slot. Suddenly a holographic image appeared of Sandra Debonshire standing in the middle of the table. But it was of a quality none of them had seen before. If they hadn't known better they would have all sworn that the young woman was actually standing in front of them on the table.

"Congratulations," she said, her voice soft but perfectly audible.

Dale started to speak, but then a foolish expression crossed her face, and she remained silent.

"Since you are viewing this disc I will assume you have somehow successfully destroyed the Citadel II Mech ship. You have bought us precious time, which we will use to prepare our defense."

The woman paused a moment, and she looked over her shoulder at something. The image seemed to waver and go out of focus, but then it solidified again, and when she turned back she seemed like a totally different person from a moment ago. She seemed worried now, almost frightened, and there was a haunted look in her eyes.

"Something has happened . . . ," she started, but then she stopped in midsentence to look over her shoulder again. When she turned back she reached forward, her hand disappearing in front of her, and when she straightened up the worry on her face was even more intense than before.

"What's happening?" Dale asked, but before Flash could answer her, Sandra's image continued.

"An hour has elapsed since I made the first portion of this message, and in that time something has occurred that none of us at Citadel I dreamed was possible."

She reached forward again to do something with her hand beyond the range of the image pickup, and then she looked directly at Flash seated in her chair.

"I must leave immediately, so I will have to be quick about this. Please listen very carefully to what I am about to say."

Flash sat forward in his chair. Whatever had happened to her must have been important. He only hoped that she would leave them at least a clue to where she had gone.

"There are no weapons of any use to us here in this museum. I know that now, although I do not understand it. However . . ." She hesitated a moment. "However, I have just discovered that this planet is not devoid of life. My scanners have shown lifeforms in the mountains to the north. I'm reading some kind of a low-level electrical interference. Sentient produced.

"I'm leaving immediately to try and find these people, and if you are able, please come after me."

Once again she reached forward to do something out of the pickup's range, and now the strain in her face was even greater. "Be careful," she said. "Whoever these mountain people are, they have discovered my scanners, because they have put out a powerful muting signal that has completely blocked my detectors."

The image winked out of existence, and Flash was about to reach for the disc when Sandra was back once again.

"Take the ramp up to the museum exit that the droids burned through, and to the left you will find a series of large blue plates set in the floor. Step onto the one marked with the symbol that looks like an English-language T, and you will be transmitted outside the building. I will have a groundcar with provisions waiting there for you."

She stepped forward a couple of paces and held both hands out almost as if she was pleading with them.

"Dr. Zarkov, Col. Gordon, Dale, I need your help, more now than ever before. I'm heading due north into the mountains. The last reading I managed to take put the electrical interference about four hundred kilometers distant.

"These people, whoever they are, may be the creators of this place, or at least their descendants. If that is so, they may be our only hope of survival. But be careful."

The image faded and died, and this time the message disc popped out of its slot.

Flash sat back in the chair, and after a moment he looked up at Zarkov and Dale, who were staring at him.

Dale seemed to be holding her breath, her complexion a pasty white, but Zarkov shook his head.

"Do we have any other choice?" the old man asked. There was excitement in his voice.

"None," Flash said. He pushed the chair back and got to his feet. The control panel slid neatly back into the tabletop and was gone without a trace.

Like everything else they had done since leaving Earth, there had been no choice. They had been pushed along one direct line of action, but where it was taking them he could not even guess.

CHAPTER 11

It took them nearly twenty minutes to make it all the way to the top of the assembly hall and find the proper matter transmitter plate Sandra had described for them, but in less than a second they were transported to the building's main entrance.

As promised, a groundcar was parked just outside the building near the charred remains of their hovershuttle.

Flash helped Zarkov down the single step, across the mall to the groundcar, and then into one of the rear contour seats.

Zarkov was nearly collapsed with fatigue—he was simply too old for these exertions—and Flash decided that he was not going to allow the old man to come up into the mountains. Besides the strenuousness of the trip, there was a very good chance they would run into trouble. Trouble that the old man simply was not equipped to handle.

They would have to return to the spaceport, and

although it would be much quicker for them to return through the portal from the government assembly hall, Zarkov was not up to that trip either.

"We're going back to the spaceport first, and I'm going to drop you off at the ship, Hans," Flash said.

Dale had found the provisions Sandra had left for them in a compartment behind the rear seats of the vehicle, and she looked up and nodded her approval.

Zarkov started to protest. "I must go with you . . ."

"You'll do us more good back at the ship," Flash interrupted gently. "I have a feeling that sooner or later we're going to have to get out of here in a big hurry. But until the ship's systems have been figured out, it won't be much use to us in an emergency."

Flash could see that Zarkov understood the logic of his argument, but the old man continued to protest.

"If Miss Debonshire is correct and those people up there are the descendants of the builders of this place, their worth could be inestimable."

"We'll find out what we can, Doc," Flash said. "Meanwhile we still may need some way of getting off this planet in a big hurry." He looked into his old friend's eyes, and he could see something of the pain and frustration the aging scientist was feeling. Despite the Federation's advanced science, and despite the technology of the Citadel's computer, Zarkov was still an old man. His muscles were weak, his body soft. There was nothing to be done about it. Despite what the old man wanted to do, deep in his heart he understood Flash was correct. He finally acquiesced.

"Be careful," he said.

Dale had come around from the rear of the groundcar, and she handed her uncle several of the containers, which held food and drink similar to the provisions they had subsisted on during their stay on Citadel I.

"She must have gotten this stuff from the museum," Dale said. She climbed in the front passenger seat, and Flash slid in behind the control column, which operated the small gravity-resist generator, propulsion and braking motors, and steering mechanism.

"This groundcar too," he said. "Its design is almost exactly the same as the ones on Citadel I."

As soon as Flash touched the control column the groundcar came to life, rising a few centimeters off the pavement. Soon they were racing down the wide, deserted boulevard, heading due south toward the spaceport at the edge of the city.

Between huge buildings, whose spires were lost in the early-afternoon sky; beneath the spidery walkways, some high up but others only a half-dozen meters overhead; past fountains and statuary depicting things or ideas they could not even begin to guess at; and past broad intersections where once traffic had teemed, they sped away from the Government Center, which at one time had not only been the center of the city, but the center of all life in the galaxy as well.

The trip took a couple of hours, which gave Dale and Zarkov time to eat and drink from the provisions and manage to snatch a few minutes' sleep.

Finally the broad roadway on which they traveled curved to the left and ended in a ramp leading down to the spaceport. In the distance to the east they could see the Citadel II warship they had stolen, gleaming black against the pale blue spaceport surface, and Flash turned the groundcar that way.

By the time they had retraced their path back to the government center, Sandra would have had a half-day's headstart, and Flash only hoped that they would somehow be able to pick up her trail. She was a biological robot under the control of the Citadel I computer, and she had used and manipulated them to this point; yet Flash found it difficult to think of her in those terms. To him, and he was sure to Dale and Zarkov as well, she was in truth Sandra Debonshire, a young woman who was twenty-two years old, and who would always be twenty-two. They could not leave her here.

Besides, Flash thought, if they were to get anything, anything at all, from this city to help them fight the machines of Citadel II, they would need her help.

He pulled up smoothly alongside the warship's open ramp, jumped out of the groundcar, and helped Zarkov from the back seat.

Dale took a portion of the provisions and carried them aboard the ship, as Zarkov and Flash hesitated a moment by the hatch.

Zarkov looked north in the direction of the unseen mountains. "You've got a long trip ahead of you. It's more than six hundred kilometers to the edge of the mountain range, and there is no telling how far up you'll have to go." He turned to look at Flash. "Be careful," he said with much emotion.

"You too," Flash said.

Dale came out of the ship and pecked her uncle on the cheek. "Try to get some rest," she said.

He nodded and smiled tiredly. "If you're not back here within twenty-four hours, I'll start a life-forms scan."

"They muted Sandra's scanners," Dale said.

"I can pinpoint the muting signal, and I'll follow it in with the ship."

"Get some sleep first, Hans," Flash said.

"I'll try. Good luck."

From the air Flash had seen that the city was divided into four quadrants by two main avenues —one running north-south and the other east-west, both meeting at the government center. They headed back along the north-south avenue directly toward the huge pyramidal building. Once they had made it that far they would have to take a side street to get around the structure until they could again pick up the north-south boulevard and continue toward the mountains.

But what lay beyond the city's edge remained to be seen. If the long-gone inhabitants of Centrus took trips by groundcar into the countryside, there would be highways. If, on the other hand, they traveled outside the city only by air or by matter transmitter, the mountains would be a wilderness, and they would have to continue on foot.

For the first twenty minutes from the spaceport they were silent, studying with wonder the vast city they were speeding through.

The thought kept occurring to Flash, as he drove, that there was so much here that they did not understand, that they could never possibly hope to understand in a hundred lifetimes. And yet it occurred to him that perhaps the original inhabi-

tants of this place had no more understanding of it
than he did. Despite their vast knowledge, they had
not been able to avoid a devastating war that had
annihilated a once-fabulous civilization.

At least back home, in their fledgling Federation, they had somehow managed to avoid war
since the twentieth century. There were occasional
uprisings and crime, of course, but all-out war was
a thing of the past. Through generation after generation, the very thought of such a struggle was being
bred out of the human race.

Why, he asked himself, couldn't a civilization so
advanced as this one avoid war? Why?

"If the war came here to Centrus, why wasn't the
city destroyed?" Dale asked suddenly. She evidently had been thinking along the same lines as Flash.

He glanced at her. "I don't know," he said.
"There is some damage at the spaceport, but
you're right, nothing was destroyed here in the
city."

"And where did the people go?"

"Some to Citadel I. Others to the mountains."

"You'd think that after twenty thousand years
they would have come back to the city. My God,
that's time enough for a dozen civilizations to
spring up, develop, and revive this technology."

"Maybe they built up a religion with powerful
taboos against the city. Maybe this is holy
ground."

"Or unholy ground," Dale said, and she shuddered at the thought.

It was late afternoon by the time they reached
the Government Center, and without hesitation
Flash took one of the side streets that paralleled

the wall surrounding the building.

Within ten minutes they had come to the opposite side of the building, and once again they sped north along the main thoroughfare toward the mountains and whatever awaited them there.

After an hour or so, Flash let Dale drive while he crawled in the back seat, ate and drank, and then lay back for some much needed rest. But his sleep was fitful, and he kept dreaming first about fighting the Citadel II warrior droids, and then trying without success to defend a woman against their attack. But the woman kept changing from Dale to his wife and back to Dale again, so that he was never quite sure who she was.

When he finally awoke the sun had dropped below the horizon, and although it was technically nighttime on this planet, the light from the myriad of stars in the sky made it seem like day, only without the shadows cast by the sun.

Dale had stopped the groundcar on the approach ramp of a huge bridge that spanned a gorge through which a wide river raged.

The city ended abruptly at the gorge, and on the other side were heavily wooded foothills that rose in steep tiers toward the mountains, which were clearly visible in the distance.

Flash got out of the groundcar and stretched as Dale moved over to the passenger side, and then he climbed in behind the control column.

"How do you feel?" she asked.

"Better," Flash said. His side was stiff but the wound was healing well, and now that he had eaten and had gotten at least a little sleep, he felt much refreshed.

The groundcar's gravity-resist generator

hummed softly, the noise barely audible over the roar of the river below them. The night had become cool, but not as cold as they expected it would because of the relatively thin atmosphere, and there was little or no wind. But Flash could smell the trees, and that brought another thought.

He turned in his seat to look back toward the city, which gleamed softly in the bright starlight. Dale followed his gaze.

"What is it?" she asked.

He looked at her. "Part of the mystery has just been solved, I think."

Her eyebrows knitted. "What do you mean?"

"I think I know why the mountain people never reinhabited the city."

She glanced back again the way they had come, but said nothing.

"Nothing lives back there. No grass, no trees, no plants of any sort. No insects. No rodents. Nothing."

Understanding dawned on Dale's face, and she turned to look across the river at the heavily wooded foothills. "Something killed every living thing in the city, but left the buildings intact."

Flash nodded. "And whatever it was evidently sterilized the city for good."

Dale shuddered. "What about us?"

"It's too late now to worry about it," he said. "Besides, if it was going to affect us, it would already have happened."

She looked at him doubtfully, and he turned away, not at all sure that what he had told her was true, except for the fact that it was probably too late to worry about it.

Again he seriously wondered if they would ever get out of here, or if they did, if they would ever finally return home. But he shook that thought away and pushed the control column forward. The groundcar moved smoothly up the approach ramp and across the bridge.

The highway across the river narrowed and wound its way through the ever-rising foothills in the strange night light that made everything appear flat, without depth.

Unlike the city, here the roadway was littered with debris, and Flash had to slow down to avoid collisions. Many trees were dead and down, and in one spot a small stream flowed directly across the highway. When their groundcar passed over it, a wide spray of water spewed to both sides, the vehicle shuddering from the sudden resistance.

Then for a long stretch, at least fifty kilometers, the roadway was fairly clear, and they were able to make good time. Sandra had told them she was heading due north out of the city, and that was the road they had taken. She also had told them that the signals her scanner had detected were four hundred kilometers away from the government center. At this point they had traveled well over three hundred kilometers, and as best Flash could estimate, four hundred kilometers would put them well into the mountain range they were entering.

The countryside was rugged. Tall trees, reminiscent of pine trees back on Earth, crowded the steep ravines, and in the valleys smaller, gnarled trees competed with thick underbrush for sunlight and water.

Although the mountains were tall, their peaks

bare, they were more rounded, more weathered, than the Rockies or the Himalayas on Earth, and probably much older.

Everything they had seen on this planet, from the spaceport terminals to the city itself and now the countryside, seemed ancient and somehow used up. It was almost as if the inhabitants of this place had consumed all of its resources, including its beauty, and then had discarded what remained.

They came around a wide sweeping curve onto a straightaway that was clear for several kilometers, as the road rose even higher toward a pass through the first of the mountains. Flash gently eased the control column forward, and the groundcar accelerated.

If Sandra had any hope of being found, she would have left them some kind of sign along the road. As he drove he watched the roadside for anything that might indicate where she had stopped. Rocks piled up, a piece of metal or cloth—anything out of the ordinary.

They topped the rise, and the road dipped down again and curved sharply to the left. They were going a little too fast, so Flash eased back on the control column. At that instant he saw a huge tree lying directly in their path.

Dale screamed as he hauled the control column all the way back, exerting the maximum braking force, and slammed it to the right, slewing the vehicle sideways, its motors screaming and its gravity-resist generator howling against the heavy load being imposed on it.

At the last moment, before the rear of their groundcar crashed into the outstretched branches,

Flash reached out with his right arm and pushed
Dale down, below the level of the windscreen, and
then threw his body over hers to cushion the blow.

The vehicle skidded sideways up a large branch,
then spun around, metal screeching and tearing.
The gravity-resist generator finally burned out with
a loud snap, and then they came to rest, half over
on their side, the rear of the groundcar butted up
against the trunk of the huge tree.

Flash's heart was hammering against his chest,
his adrenaline pumping, as he sat up and helped
Dale back up into the seat.

"Are you all right?" he asked anxiously.

She shook her head as if to clear it. "I think so,"
she said in a weak voice. There was a small welt on
her forehead, and she reached up to touch it and
winced.

"No broken bones?"

She looked up at him and smiled uncertainly.
"I'm okay," she said. "How about you?"

"Fine," he said absently, relieved that neither of
them had been seriously injured. He pushed himself up so that he was standing on the seat, and
tried to look over the tree trunk, but he could not
get high enough.

One thing he was certain of, however. This tree
had not been here when Sandra passed. It was new-
ly felled. And unless he missed his bet, it had not
fallen naturally. It had been cut down.

"We've got to get out of here," he said. He
helped Dale up.

"What about the groundcar?"

"I heard the gravity-resist generator pop just
before we hit," Flash said. "We're going to have to

walk." He stepped over the shattered windscreen onto the groundcar's hood, pushing aside several branches, but Dale held back.

"This tree isn't dead," she said. "It didn't just fall down."

"That's right," Flash snapped. "Now come on, we've got to get out of here before whoever cut it down decides to return and see what they've caught."

He reached out again for her hand when something hard slammed into his back, shoving him forward. An instant later what felt like a battering ram smashed into the back of his head. The last thing he was conscious of was Dale's scream.

CHAPTER 12

Flash never remembered much of his journey into the mountains that night. Time for him consisted of periods of intense pain, punctuated by dim moments of semiconsciousness.

He was aware only vaguely that his hands and feet were tightly bound, and that he was lying over some kind of an animal that moved and bounced and shivered beneath his weight. At times he was also aware that they seemed to be climbing vertical walls, and that the tiny section of ground he could see directly beneath the animal was rocky and totally devoid of any plantlife.

His head was on fire and throbbed painfully with each heartbeat. At least one of his ribs seemed to be broken, and his hands and feet were numb from where the cords binding him had cut off the circulation.

During his rare periods of semi lucidness, he held the single hope that Dale had not been treated as roughly as he had been, and with that thought a dark anger welled up inside of him.

But then he would lose consciousness again, and when he awoke he would go through all the same thoughts, feelings, and impressions. It was as if each time he passed out, his mind was erased of all previous knowledge.

The sun was just coming up over the mountains when at long last the arduous journey was completed, and Flash could feel strong hands pulling him from the animal he had been tied to. He fell to the ground, where he lay on his back trying to focus his eyes. He could just make out several figures looming over him, and then they moved away.

A minute or an hour later, he had no idea which, the cords binding him were cut, and he was dragged across the ground into some kind of a rude hut with a dirt floor, and then he was hoisted up onto a low bed, the pain from his head and chest injuries so excruciating that he cried out.

A blanket was thrown over him, and his world went dim once again as the pain blissfully receded.

Several times during the day and into the second night Flash became aware that someone was holding his shoulders, lifting him upright, and making him drink a bitter liquid.

The drink made him gag, but immediately afterward a soft, warm feeling of well-being spread throughout his body. His aches and sharp pains were soothed, and he would then drop again into a dreamless sleep.

How many times that routine was repeated he could not tell, but finally he awoke, aware that he was lying on a cot, a blanket covering his body, bandages around his head and around his chest. Through the open door of the hut he could see that it was strangely dark outside.

He pushed away the cover and sat up, the action causing a sharp pain in his back and a period of intense dizziness and nausea. But this passed quickly and he was able to swing his legs over the side of the bed.

He was naked, but in the dim light thrown by a single oil lamp across the small room from him, he could see his white coveralls and boots neatly placed on some kind of a wooden chest.

He got up from the bed and slowly made his way across the room. He pulled on his clothes, which he found had been laundered. When he was dressed, he turned around.

A man stood in the doorway to the hut. He was a good head taller than Flash, but thin, with dark skin, black hair, and narrow, dark eyes. He was dressed in what appeared to be an animal hide jerkin and leggings, and buckled around his waist was an ornately decorated wide belt and a scabbard containing a short sword like the one Flash had taken from the armory at the spaceport terminal tower.

What was most striking about the man, however, were his arms and legs, which seemed to have no joints. His hands were long and delicate, and even in the dim light Flash could see they had six digits. He was one of the descendants of the inhabitants of Centrus.

"The starman awakens," the man said, his voice soft, almost liquid. He spoke in the language Martin had taught them all back on Citadel I, although he spoke it with an odd, lilting accent.

"My companion," Flash said, his voice cracked. "Where is she?"

The man just looked at Flash, his eyes unblinking, as if he had not heard or understood what was being said to him.

Flash took a step forward, and with lightning speed the man had the short sword out of his scabbard and held it in his left hand, the point down, at least for the moment.

"Where is the woman who came with me?" Flash said carefully. "Do you understand what I am saying?"

"Come," the man said. "Your trial begins." He turned and went out the door.

Flash did not move from his spot, and a moment later the man was back.

"Come, starman."

Still Flash did not move. "I will not, until you tell me where the woman is being held."

The man seemed to contemplate what Flash had asked him, and then he inclined his head slightly and blinked. "The two females are at the council fire. You will come with me, and I will take you to them."

Once again the man turned, and with inhuman grace and agility he was out the door. This time Flash followed him outside, where he found that they were halfway up one side of a wide, shallow valley ringed with huge trees whose branches intertwined far overhead, almost completely blocking out the sky. That explained why it was dark outside, and looking up Flash could just make out the stars through the branches as brilliant points of light. It was nighttime, but he wondered which night. How long had they been captive? And what was Zarkov doing at this moment?

"Come, starman," the man said again, and he headed down into the valley, which was studded with hundreds of wooden huts of various sizes and shapes, toward a large campfire far below.

Flash followed the man as best he could, and after a few moments the man trotted back up the hill.

"Faster," he said.

Flash shook his head slowly. "I cannot," he said, and he maintained his steady pace down the hill.

The man shifted his weight from one foot to the other, a gesture of impatience or agreement, Flash could not know which, but finally he moved ahead to lead the way, though at a much slower pace.

Near the bottom of the valley was a series of wide, low buildings behind which was a fenced area where a large number of animals were contentedly grazing. They looked very much like Earth horses, only they were taller, and like the man their legs seemed spindly and totally devoid of any joints.

As he walked, Flash studied the layout of the camp, especially the paths that led up the valley and into the forests above. If they could somehow steal weapons and three of the horses, they might have a chance, however slight, of escape.

But that thought was pushed to the back of his mind instantly as they came around one of the buildings and he spotted Dale and Sandra seated on fur hides around the large fire. At least two hundred people of the same race as Flash's escort were also seated around the fire.

Dale turned, and when she saw Flash she started

to jump up. "Flash!" she cried. But two of the men
seated behind her and Sandra roughly pulled her
back down.

"No!" Flash shouted, and he leaped forward.

His escort put out a hand to try and stop him,
but a blackness welled up inside of Flash, and he
smashed his right fist into the man's face, which
erupted in a mass of blood and bone.

A collective roar rose from the crowd, and before
Flash could take two steps there were a dozen men
on top of him, shoving him down, pinning his arms
and legs to the ground.

He struggled wildly a few seconds longer, but it
was useless, and he willed his entire body to go
limp.

The men holding him down let go and got up
after several long seconds, allowing Flash to get
painfully to his feet. He found that he was surrounded by a dozen drawn swords.

For a moment he considered trying to break out
of the circle, but then decided against it. They were
weak, but they were too fast, and there were too
many of them.

"Come," one of the men said, and the circle
parted so that he could proceed to where Dale and
Sandra were seated.

He glanced back at the man he had struck down.
There was nothing left of his head but a bloody
pulp, and his left leg was twitching violently. No
one seemed to notice their fallen comrade, however, or even care about him.

Flash turned and went through the circle to Dale
and Sandra, and several of the men shoved him
down beside the women on a large fur hide.

"Oh God . . . Flash darling . . . I didn't know what was happening to you . . . they wouldn't tell me a thing," Dale blurted.

"No talking," one of the men behind them hissed.

"Are you all right?" Flash asked, keeping his voice low. The bruise on her forehead from the groundcar accident had grown larger, and she instinctively reached up to touch it.

She nodded. "They didn't hurt me."

"No talking," one of their captors repeated, but Flash ignored him. He turned to Sandra, who was staring impassively at the fire. "Sandra?" he said, touching her arm.

She turned slowly to look at him, but her face was totally devoid of emotion or expression.

"She's been like that since we got here . . . ," Dale started to say, when one of the men behind them cuffed her on the side of the head.

Flash leaped backward into the midst of a half-dozen men, swinging and slamming his fists with all his might, like a wild man. Before he was once again subdued, he counted at least three of them down.

He was dragged roughly back onto the fur hide, his heart hammering wildly, and this time before his arms were released, a sword was pressed against the back of his neck.

"Move and you die, starman," the man holding the sword said close to his ear.

"Don't touch the girl and you'll have no more resistance from me," Flash said loudly. The blackness inside of him was just beneath the surface, ready to break through at the smallest provocation. It was all he could do to hold himself in check. The sword was withdrawn after a moment. "Agreed," the man behind him said.

"Mother comes," someone on the other side of the fire shouted. A moment later someone else shouted the same two words, and soon the entire crowd took up the chant: "Mother comes! Mother comes! Mother comes!"

Flash started to turn toward Sandra, when a brilliant burst of light exploded from the center of the large fire. When it died away, an incredibly old and frail-looking woman of the same race as their captors stood a few meters in front of them. Unlike the others, who were clad in animal hides, the old woman was dressed in a dazzlingly white, full-length robe with a brilliant red sash tied around her middle. Her left hand supported a tall staff that appeared to Flash to be made of white plasti steel.

The crowd had fallen silent, and only the crackling and popping of the logs on the fire broke the still night air as the ancient crone glided smoothly forward as if she was riding on a gravity-resist pad.

She stopped a half-meter away, looked imperiously down at Flash, and then turned slowly so that she faced the majority of her people gathered around the fire.

"It was written at the dawn of time when we were driven from the forbidden city that the destroyers would come," the woman said. She spoke in a clear, well-modulated voice that carried no trace of the accent her people spoke with.

"These destroyers would be men of the stars, different from us in appearance and purpose. They would come riding down on pillars of fire, bringing with them the old ways. Bringing with them the war that drove from our midst our finest citizens.

"It was written at the dawn of time that the destroyers would come to the forbidden city by the great blue plain along the sea, and that they would plunder the secrets hidden there. That they would violate the mysteries that are preserved within for our old ones."

She turned slowly so that she was once again staring down at Flash. "These, then, are the destroyers come finally among us, as it was written. These then are the violators of the old ones' technologies, come here to activate the great *Ultimus* of the South."

"Death!" someone on the other side of the fire shouted loudly.

"Death to the destroyers!" someone else shouted, and soon the new chant was taken up by the crowd, but Flash was watching Sandra, who had suddenly come out of her almost hypnotic trance.

"That's it," she said softly, the words barely forming on her lips. She turned excitedly toward Flash and Dale, her eyes alight. "The *Ultimus*," she said urgently. "That's what we came here for! Martin wasn't sure it even existed. But it does! It does!"

"What are you talking about?" Dale started to ask, but the chanting of the crowd was getting louder now, reduced to a single word.

"Death! Death! Death!" the crowd repeated over and over again in an ominous rhythm that grew in intensity and speed.

The old woman in front of them was striking the

base of her staff on the ground in time with the
rhythm of the chant, when a narrow beam of light
shot from the other end of it, straight up through
the overhanging branches far above them.

Even over the roar of the crowd around them
Flash was certain he could hear the characteristic
hum of a fairly powerful laser device, and before
anyone could stop him, he leaped up and grabbed
the staff from the old woman, swinging it with both
hands like a club, the laser beam slashing the air
just above the crowd.

A half-dozen of the men, swords in hand,
jumped up from where they were seated and raced
toward Flash. He lowered the angle of the staff,
and the laser beam sliced through their bodies,
which fell writhing in the dust, the stench of
cooked meat nauseating.

The old woman, screaming and babbling now,
shrank back, but Flash quickly turned the laser
lance her way, holding the beam just above her
head.

"Stop or your leader dies!" he shouted at the top
of his lungs.

Several of the men advanced around the fire
from behind him. Dale cried out, "Behind you,
Flash!"

He half-turned toward them, then quickly
shifted his attention back to the old woman and
brought the laser beam closer to her head. She
shrieked.

"She will die!" he shouted.

The crowd fell silent, and the hum of the laser
device in Flash's hands was loud now.

After several long seconds one of the men seated

near Dale and Sandra carefully laid his sword on the ground and then stepped away from the circle of people so that he stood alone, several meters away from Flash and the old woman.

"What do you want of us?" he said, his voice choked with emotion.

"A clear way out of here," Flash snapped.

"We cannot allow it," the man said.

"Then your Mother will die."

"No," the man said, holding both of his hands out, palms up. "I beseech you. No."

"Sandra," Flash shouted, without taking his eyes off the old woman or the man, and she and Dale got to their feet.

"Yes?" she said.

"What is this *Ultimus* you spoke of? What is it?"

"It's the ultimate weapon that was supposed to end the war for all times," she said.

The man standing swordless in front of Flash looked with wonder at Sandra.

"Martin and the computer weren't sure it even existed. It was supposedly in the developmental stage when the end came here, and the creators fled to Citadel I. It was the most closely guarded secret of the entire galaxy."

"Is it transportable?" Flash asked.

"I don't know," she said. "Martin didn't even know. But if it exists we must have it at all costs. It would assure peace."

"What do you know of this?" Flash asked the man.

"I know nothing, only Mother knows," the man said. He seemed confused, and he kept glancing from Flash to Sandra and back to Flash again.

"But you are the destroyers. The others."

"No," Flash said. "We are of your old ones' world. A world they created when they left this planet."

"It cannot be," the man cried, stepping back.

Flash turned again to the old woman, who was cringing beneath the laser beam. "Where is this *Ultimus*?" he asked her, but she could only mumble incoherently. "I will kill your people one by one until you tell me," he shouted.

"No," Dale screamed, and she rushed up behind him. "You can't do that, Flash. These are innocent people."

"Who would have killed us."

"Only because they thought we were their enemy," Dale argued. She was crying. "For God's sake, Flash, you can't murder innocent men and women."

She was right, of course. There was no way possible he could murder innocent people. He raised the staff straight up so that the laser beam was pointing away and found the cut-off switch, which was nothing more than a twist sleeve near the base. The beam died with a snap.

"We are not your enemy," Flash said to the crowd. "We are not the destroyers that you have been waiting for, but we have done battle with them. Even at this moment they are preparing to come here and destroy the great city. When they have accomplished that, they will come to the planet that your old ones created and destroy it as well. And then they will rule the galaxy. Every star, every planet, every people will be theirs."

No one moved, no one made a noise. The old

woman had recovered somewhat, and she gazed at Flash without expression.

"*Ultimus*, if it exists, is our only hope for survival. You must help us find it."

The man who had put his weapon down stepped forward. "It is in a city to the south, in the Great Equator Desert. I know nothing else."

The old woman reached inside her robe, and before Flash could do a thing to stop her, she withdrew a short sword and leaped forward, swinging the blade, splitting the man's body from his breast bone to his hips.

"Death to the destroyers!" she screamed, and the crowd went into a frenzy.

CHAPTER 13

The old woman spun on her left foot with surprising speed and agility for her age, and swung the sword directly at Flash's middle.

He tried to fend off the blow with the staff, but the blade cut cleanly through it amid a shower of sparks, and she raised the sword again for the death cut, when the trees overhead exploded in a ball of fire, causing burning branches to rain down atop the crowd.

The woman looked up, and at that instant Flash leaped forward, wrestled the sword from her hand, and grabbed her frail body, pulling her around so that he had her neck in a tight grip.

"The destroyers," the crowd screamed, and Flash looked up as a black Citadel II warship turned gracefully over on its side and descended slowly toward them through the blasted opening in the trees.

Everyone scattered, racing away from the council fire, some of the men even dropping their weapons. The old woman in Flash's grip screamed and cried and struggled wildly against him, froth coming to her lips and her eyes wide with absolute, insane terror.

Flash let her go, and hiking up her skirts, she made a mad dash away from the council fire, as the warship loomed huge a few meters overhead, and the hatch slid open.

"Come on," Flash shouted, as the ship eased a little lower.

Sandra and Dale raced across the clearing, and he helped them climb up through the hatch, onto the steeply sloping deck.

Zarkov was at the controls, and when he saw they were all aboard, he rotated the ship on its roll axis so that the deck was more level, and Flash managed to hit the airlock cycle button. The hatch slid shut.

"Strap down," Zarkov shouted, as the ship began to climb. Flash helped Dale and Sandra into acceleration couches, then went forward and slid into a seat next to Zarkov's.

A moment later Zarkov's fingers played over the control panel, and the ship shot straight up, pressing them into their seats.

"I was never so glad to see anyone in all my life," Flash shouted over the howl of the reaction engines.

Zarkov glanced over at him and shook his head. He looked white with exhaustion and fear. "You won't say that when you see what's in store for us."

"What is it, Doc?"

"Just a minute and you'll see," Zarkov shouted.

The ship continued to climb, its rate of acceleration building, until they achieved orbit about a thousand kilometers out. Zarkov cut the engines. To the east they could see the terminator area of the approaching dawn, a golden color against the sea.

Zarkov did something with one of the controls, and the forward view area changed into a grid map with thousands of red specks, obviously moving in formation.

"We're on long-range hyperspace scanner now," Zarkov said in a hushed tone. "It's showing an area of space less than a light year distant. I think it's a staging point. Before long they'll all make the jump, and they'll be on top of us."

"Citadel II?" Flash asked, stunned.

Zarkov nodded. "I would have come sooner, but one of their advanced scouts dropped in on me at the spaceport yesterday just before I was going to come looking for you. I had to jump into energy drive directly from ground level. Made quite a hole in the ground. By the time I came back into real space I had no idea where I was. It took me the better part of twenty hours to figure out the onboard astrogation equipment and then come up with a reasonable fix. Even then I had to make a half-dozen jumps before I figured out the controls well enough to make the fine adjustments."

"How'd you find us?" Flash asked.

Zarkov stared at the scanner for several long moments, apparently deep in thought, before he once again looked down. "When I finally got back to the port, the scout was gone, and I started an immediate lifeforms scan, which intercepted the muting signal. I followed that up into the mountains but couldn't pinpoint the specific location until I saw a laser signal coming out of the trees. I homed in on that, and using infrared scans, I picked up the fire and body-head readings." He glanced up at the scanner, then back at Flash. "What happened down there? Are you all right? Did you come up with anything that can help us out of this situation?"

"We're fine, now," Flash said. "And I think we may have come up with something, but it's probably a long shot. I don't know if we're going to have enough time."

Now that their position was stabilized, Sandra and Dale were able to come forward.

"We must have the time," Sandra said. She too looked up at the scanner. "If they're allowed to take over here, we're done."

Zarkov looked around at her and shook his head. "There isn't much we're going to be able to do with this one ship," he said. "Unless you've got something else in your bag of tricks."

"I hope so," she said absently. Then she looked directly into Zarkov's eyes. "Take us down to around ten thousand meters directly over the planet's equator. There's supposed to be a city in the desert."

Zarkov looked uncertainly to Flash, who nodded, and a moment later the aging scientist adjusted the controls. The warship began to fall planetside, the gravity-resist generators easily taking up the decelerative shock. He flipped the forward view area back to optical, and the planet came into view, the great sea spread out below them.

Far to the east, however, toward the rising sun, they could just make out a light brown land mass, and Sandra excitedly pointed that way.

"There," she said, and Zarkov headed the ship that way.

"How long do we have left?" Flash asked.

Zarkov glanced up at him. "I don't know. If they made the jump now, and they were all flying the matter-energy drives, I'd say a few hours. But there's no way of telling when they're going to come in. Their scout encountered resistance from me, so they'll be prepared for a fight."

Flash turned to Sandra, who was staring intently out the forward view area, watching as the light brown land mass rose up to meet them from the sea. When she became aware that he was looking at her, she glanced up, her eyes meeting his.

"How much more did Martin tell you about this weapon?" he asked.

She shook her head slowly. "I've told you everything."

He reached out and grabbed her arm. "Our life depends upon this, Sandra!"

"I'm telling you the truth," she cried.

"If you are, it will be the first time since we met you," he said, tightening his grip on her tiny arm.

She tried to struggle away from him. "You're hurting me," she said.

"Flash?" Dale said uncertainly.

"You're a droid, Sandra, under the control of Martin and the computer. What else do you know about this *Ultimus*?"

The young woman's eyes were wide with fright, and Zarkov and Dale were both watching Flash, not understanding what he was doing. It was unlike him to inflict this kind of pain on anyone without good purpose.

"Yes," Sandra snapped. "I am a droid, a biological robot. But I would challenge any medical man or automed in the galaxy to distinguish me now from the body I was born with. I hurt, I bleed, and I have feelings just like before."

Flash let go, suddenly feeling very tired and confused. He did not know what to believe any longer. She had lied to them all along. She had maneuvered them into their present position with a machine-like efficiency, and yet now he wanted to believe that she did indeed hurt and have normal human feelings.

"I'm sorry," he mumbled.

Sandra reached out and gently touched his cheek with her fingertips. "I'm sorry too, Col. Gordon, for everything that you and Dale and Dr. Zarkov have been through, but we need your help." She looked up at the forward view area as they came over the coastline of the desert, which stretched inland to the horizon.

"We're over the equator," Zarkov said softly, checking his instruments. "What specifically are we looking for?"

"I don't know," Sandra replied. "A city, a machine, something sentient-built out on the desert." She turned again to look at Flash, and an expression of sadness crossed her features. "Don't judge us too harshly, Col. Gordon. We all believe in what we've done, what we've become." She ran her fingers through her hair. "You must understand that when we headed out from Earth, we all were starry-eyed idealists. We were going on the greatest adventure in the history of the human race. We were headed to the stars. We were leaving our families and friends behind, knowing full well that we would never see them again. Ours was to be a one-way trip. We all knew that when we signed on and started our training."

"You don't have to tell us all that," Dale started, but the young woman cut her off.

"No, Dale, you're wrong. You all deserve an explanation," she said, and she turned once again to face Flash. "The Citadel I computer is paranoid, if a machine can have such a human condition. Its primal circuits were set up to fear and mistrust offworlders. The war had been dormant for twenty thousand years, and the galaxy was finally beginning to heal itself. But then the Goodhope was launched about the same time Citadel II began its first exploratory probes of our corner of the galaxy.

"The computer was running out of options. It is only a machine and can accomplish only so much. It is only a repository of knowledge, not a sentient creature.

"So Martin came out to get us. He explained everything, and we all agreed to help. Every one of us, without a single dissenting vote, agreed to help. My God, it's exactly the mission we were sent out on: populate the galaxy, spread the seed of man with the message of peace. Unless Citadel II is defeated there never can be such a thing as peace. Nor can there be any place in the galaxy safe for mankind."

"What about us?" Flash asked. "Why were we brought into it?"

Sandra shook her head. "After 120 years we began to stagnate. We began to think more and more like the computer, and less and less like growing, living human beings. You saw that in Peter. He was affected by the machine more than any of us for some reason. We were and still are unable to bear children and populate the planet. Yet we needed new life to continue the struggle," she said bitterly.

"Why didn't you contact Earth?" Dale asked.

Sandra turned to her and smiled wistfully. "Could you guarantee, absolutely guarantee, the peaceful intentions of the entire human race when faced with the possibilities our technology offers?"

Dale started to speak, but then held off. After a long moment she shook her head.

"No," Sandra said. "Perhaps someday, but not yet."

"Meanwhile, Citadel II had come up with a new and unexpected technology," Flash said.

Sandra nodded. "We saw it coming with the scout ship that scanned us fifty years ago. Our computer-extrapolated model of what a Citadel II scout ship should be capable of was slightly off. It was the first serious anomaly in the predictions.

"Then the matter-energy drive came so totally as a surprise, we all became desperate. There was nothing left for us to do but try to find Centrus and come up with something that would help."

"Then everything that happened to us back on Citadel I . . . Dr. Zarkov's computer search, Martin's disappearance, and our escape . . . it was all staged," Flash said.

"Yes," Sandra replied. "But it was staged not only for your benefit, but for the benefit of the computer's prime directive circuitry as well."

"And the *Ultimus*?" Flash asked.

"Martin mentioned it a couple of years ago. It was the closest he's ever come to wishful thinking. In my studies of the computer and of Centrus history, I discovered several other references to it. But always off-handed references. It was to be the ultimate weapon. It was under development or construction when the end came, but there was never an adequate explanation of why it was never used. I assume it was because the end came too soon. I don't really know."

"So even if the machine or weapon or whatever it is does exist, it may not be operational? It may only be half-constructed?" Flash asked.

"I'm afraid so, Col. Gordon," Sandra admitted. "But it was our only hope. We detected the Mech ship's progress toward the center of the galaxy, and we assumed that Citadel II somehow knew about the *Ultimus* and was searching for it as well."

Flash glanced up at the forward view area, and at the same time Zarkov snapped forward. Something strange was visible in the desert. Zarkov reached out and cranked up maximum magnification on the opticals.

Sandra looked up and gave a little cry of delight. "That's it!" she said. "It does exist."

It was huge, at least fifty kilometers in diameter, and consisted of a number of thick discs stacked atop each other and sloping sharply inward. The entire thing was topped by a huge white dome, which was shadowed by two immense shells that looked like high-energy radar dishes turned on edge.

Other, smaller shells, in pairs, were located at

various other levels, and the entire machine, if something so colossal could be called that, bristled with antennas, ports, wide hatches, balconies and walkways, and other protuberances that appeared to be laser-lance cannons.

The sight was awesome.

Zarkov had brought the ship in low, toward one of a large series of landing bays, and at the same time activated the scanning equipment. "The thing isn't functioning . . .," he started to say, but he was cut off in midsentence by an even more intimidating sight.

The two huge shells, which rose up at least ten kilometers from the floor of the desert, began swiveling their way, the interior of the huge dishes glowing red.

"We're being scanned . . .," Zarkov shouted, and Flash took over the controls. He slammed the ship into a deep dive, the gravity-resist generators whining in protest.

At the last instant, before they hit, Flash pulled the ship up, cranking in maximum gravity-resist power, and the vessel plowed into the desert with a tremendous lurch.

"Get out of here," Flash shouted, even before they were stopped. He undid his harnesses, helped Zarkov out of his seat, and together the four of them raced aft to the airlock, popped it open, and leaped out into the desert.

Flash half-dragged, half-carried Zarkov directly away from the ship, the girls right behind them, trudging through the deep, finely powdered sand.

"Flash," Dale cried at the same instant a gentle blast of heat washed over their backs and a tremendous clap of thunder rolled across the desert.

He turned in time to see the ship, or its image, appear within the larger of the two shells. Then it winked out of existence, and the glow faded and died.

They were all out of breath, and they sank down on the soft sand.

"What happened?" Dale gasped.

Flash shook his head. "It was starting to track us," he said, looking back to where they had crash-landed their ship. It was no longer there, nor was there any trace of it. "I didn't know if it was a weapon, but I didn't want to take the chance. We were aboard a Citadel II warship, and whatever is controlling that thing looked upon us as the enemy."

They all gazed at the thing rising huge from the desert less than five kilometers away. From this close the upper surface of the first disc, with the landing bays Zarkov had been heading for, was several thousand meters above them. And from here the machine looked less like a city than a mammoth ship of some kind. But it was on a scale beyond anything they had ever seen, including the awesome buildings and machinery they had seen in Centrus itself.

Sandra got slowly to her feet and stared across the desert at the thing. "*Ultimus*," she said softly. "It is a ship. The ultimate weapon." She turned toward the others. Her face was animated. "We've got to activate it. Take it back to Citadel I with us."

Zarkov was shaking his head. "It could take a lifetime just to figure out how to get aboard it."

"No," Sandra said. "It won't be any different

than the machinery on Citadel I. They were built by the same people." She looked back at the huge thing. "It's our only hope."

Flash got to his feet, and helped Zarkov and Dale up. "She's right, Hans," he said. He too glanced toward the thing. "We've run out of options anyway. There's nothing else we can do."

"It's a machine for war," Zarkov said. "Ultimate war, and nothing else."

"Peace," Sandra said, not turning around.

"Then why wasn't it used before? Why didn't the scientists who built Citadel I remain here and use this to end the war?"

"I don't know," Sandra said. "Maybe they didn't care any longer. Maybe they wanted Centrus destroyed. Maybe they thought the galaxy was finished." She turned back. "They didn't stay on Citadel I. When they had the computer built they left the galaxy for Andromeda."

"That's what frightens me," Zarkov said, looking up at the bright stars in the pale blue midmorning sky. "Perhaps this machine was left here intact just for us."

Flash understood what Zarkov was trying to say, but it seemed far-fetched and totally devoid of sanity. "They couldn't have done that," he said.

Zarkov just looked at him.

"It would be like leaving thermonuclear weapons or laser cubes lying around for a primitive tribe to stumble across."

"Yes," Zarkov said. "They ruined the galaxy, they killed each other off, they destroyed two fabulous civilizations, but they left behind the ultimate weapon for discovery by whatever seeds of a new civilization drifted this way."

"And here we are," Flash said.

"No," Sandra screamed. "The Citadel II forces are headed this way at this moment. Either we get this machine and use it to guarantee peace, or they get it and we will have lost. All of us will have lost, and that includes your own Federation."

"She's right," Dale said, and a look of intense pain and sadness crossed Zarkov's features.

"Force begets force," he said. "The ultimate weapon will spawn other ultimate weapons, or actions. Other terrible machines for our destruction."

"What do you want to do, old man?" Sandra shouted. "Turn your back on this and walk across the desert to the sea?"

"No," he said. "It's already too late for that."

"Then let us proceed," she said softly. She turned and headed across the desert toward the huge thing rising out of the desert. A moment later Flash, Zarkov, and Dale followed her.

CHAPTER 14

The desert winds over the years had pushed sand dunes against the sharply sloping base of the vast ship, which rose out of sight overhead now that they were close enough to touch it.

Just the top seam of an entry hatch was visible from where the sand had been swept away by a chance wind, and Sandra dropped to her hands and knees and began digging, trying to clear the entryway. There was an expression almost of religious ecstasy on her face as she worked, and for several long moments the others just watched her.

The sense of urgency Flash had felt on the bridge of the Citadel II warship was gone. For the moment the impending attack of the Citadel II forces gathering one light year away was forgotten.

He stepped back a few paces and looked up at the rows of ports and other protuberances that began about twenty meters overhead along the side of the otherwise seamless skin, and then he moved forward again to touch the side of the ship. It was warm and very smooth.

More importantly, in his mind, the ship's skin was not scoured or pitted by the constantly shifting sand. Surely twenty thousand years of desert sun and wind and sand would have had more effect on the ship's surfaces.

Other things they had seen suddenly came to Flash's mind as he turned to Zarkov, who stood watching Sandra clearing the hatchway. Dale had gotten down on her hands and knees and began digging as well, and Flash pulled the aging scientist aside.

"Martin told us that it had been twenty thousand years since the scientists fled this planet to begin construction of Citadel I."

Zarkov looked up at him and nodded. "Yes," he said.

Flash looked again at the ship's skin. "This hasn't been out here in the weather for twenty thousand years. In that time the wind would have buried it in sand. And the highway outside the city was nearly clogged with debris, but not twenty thousand years' worth."

Zarkov shook his head. "I thought of that almost immediately," he said. "But until very recently there has been automatic weather control on this planet. It's the only explanation for the condition of this and the city itself."

"What happened to the weather machinery then?"

Zarkov shrugged. "It wore out."

"Then they weren't infallible," Flash said.

Zarkov managed a slight smile. "Far from it. They were technological wizards, but not gods.

The very fact they could not overcome whatever drove them into a war that lasted eighty thousand years proves that."

The women had nearly cleared the hatch area of sand when Flash turned to help them. Something of Zarkov's dark mood had affected him, but he could see no way out of their present situation short of activating this ship.

If Citadel II was allowed to take over this planet, and more importantly this vessel, the galaxy would be lost.

He scrambled over the side of the sand dune and began digging with his hands. Another thought briefly crossed his mind: if they managed to defeat Citadel II, what would Martin and the Citadel I computer do with this machine? They would become the ultimate force in the galaxy. But would they be a force for good or for evil?

They had the hatch clear within a few minutes, and without hesitation Sandra ran the palm of her hand lightly across a small blue plate set flush in the ship's skin alongside the seam. The hatch slid smoothly upward into the bulkhead with a soft hiss.

The three of them stood a moment staring through the opening into a large featureless chamber that was illuminated with a soft white light. Across the room was another, similar hatch.

Zarkov had come to the edge of the sand dune, and he stood looking down at them, a troubled expression on his face. "Miss Debonshire," he said softly.

They all looked up at him, but Sandra said nothing, the beatific look in her eyes intense.

"You asked my niece if she could guarantee the

peaceful intention of all our people back on Earth. Can you guarantee the same for Citadel I?"

She pointed toward the open hatch without looking back. "This way lies peace," she said in a voice choked with emotion. "Peace for all times so that when the Earth's Federation makes it this far, there will be no danger of war."

Zarkov was about to say something else, but then shook his head and started down the steeply sloping sand. Flash hurried up to help him, and by the time they reached the bottom Sandra and Dale had already entered the ship.

When they all were inside, Sandra closed the hatch behind them, then hurried across the chamber and operated the control for the interior hatch, which opened to a wide, triangular-shaped corridor. Its apex was at least four meters overhead, and it stretched left and right into the distance, until it was lost to the curvature of the ship.

"We could be months exploring this ship," Dale said, as the four of them stepped into the corridor, which was also softly illuminated with a white light.

The hatch closed softly behind them, and without a word Sandra started down the corridor to the right, her footfalls sounding hollow and somehow out of place.

"Sandra?" Dale called after her, but the young woman continued down the corridor away from them.

Flash looked at Zarkov. "We're either committed to this or we're not, Doc. What do you think?"

Zarkov sighed deeply, the lines in his face pronounced, his eyes red-rimmed and bloodshot from lack of sleep. "We don't have a choice, Flash. None whatsoever."

Sandra had stopped fifty meters down the corridor, and she was gazing intently at something to her left, when the three of them hurried to her.

Set in the bulkhead was a wide window overlooking a huge chamber that contained a bewildering array of equipment. Much of it was reminiscent of the power equipment they had seen within the heart of the Citadel I computer, and there was no mistaking the fact that whoever built the Citadel I had also built this machine.

"This must be engineering level," Zarkov said finally. "The bridge is probably near the upper levels."

Sandra turned away from the window and nodded. "There has to be some kind of transportation."

Zarkov glanced down the corridor and then back at Flash, who could see his indecision. Finally the old man sighed deeply again, and then looked at Sandra.

"We don't have much time," he said.

She smiled. "We've already seen this ship's automatic defense systems. We're safe here."

"I don't care about this monstrosity," Zarkov snapped with uncharacteristic anger. "We've got to stop the Citadel II forces before they have a chance to damage the city, especially the Government Center and museum. Those are important, not this abomination."

Sandra's left eyebrow arched, and a moment later she turned on her heel and stalked down the corridor.

Zarkov turned to Flash. "Whatever happens, wherever we go, and whatever terrible things we have to do in the name of peace, promise me, Flash, that when it is over, when the Citadel II is defeated and there is no longer a need for this machine, you will help me destroy it."

Flash nodded. "I promise," he said, but somehow he did not think everything would work out as neatly as his old friend wanted.

They turned and without a further word hurried down the corridor after Sandra.

Every several hundred meters or so they came to another bulkhead with a hatch that led to a chamber, beyond which was another hatch in the outer skin. Zarkov theorized that these had been designed as maintenance exits.

After twenty minutes or so they came to a wide glass tube, at least three meters in diameter, that went to the left, spanning the huge chamber that held the machinery, then curved sharply upward.

Sandra was the first to step into the tube, and she was whisked rapidly away from them toward the interior of the ship.

Dale was next, then Zarkov, and finally Flash stepped from the corridor into the tube, and something tugged gently at his body. Then he was moving rapidly through the tube, but with no sensation of speed other than blurred images beyond the glass walls.

Within a few minutes he was deposited at the edge of a huge domed chamber, the awesomeness of which stunned him momentarily into inaction.

Dale and Zarkov stood a few meters apart below him, but at first he could not see where Sandra had gone, and he could do nothing other than try to comprehend what he was seeing.

The chamber was vast beyond belief, and shaped like a gigantic sphere. Far overhead the curved ceiling was clear, and he could see much of the ship's superstructure as well as the two huge defense shells towering into the pale blue sky.

Every several hundred meters, around the perimeter of the huge chamber and at the level Flash was standing, were other tubular openings, providing transport, he presumed, from all parts of the ship.

And below him, the lower part of the huge sphere was filled with tens of thousands of acceleration couches in rows and tiers, like a vast auditorium, all facing a great circular dais at the lowest part of the chamber.

The transport tube Flash had emerged from opened directly onto a wide ramp that led between the acceleration couches down the curved interior of the chamber.

Dale and Zarkov stood a few meters down the ramp, and far below them Flash could see Sandra running toward the dais.

He moved down the ramp to them, and without a word they all headed after the young woman, past row after row of deeply padded acceleration couches.

Everything seemed new, untouched, and unused, unlike the city of Centrus itself, which held an aura of vast age. And even more than the assembly hall in the government center, this chamber bespoke power. Raw. Unlimited. Power for a single purpose: destruction. Even Flash was intimidated by it all.

Nothing anywhere in the galaxy could hope to
resist this machine. And for the first time since they
had left Earth, Flash felt that they were absolutely
safe from attack here. And yet he was frightened of
what such a power as this would be used for.

By the time they came to the bottom of the
chamber Sandra was already on the dais, which
was twenty meters across and contained a number
of equipment consoles very similar in design to the
power and computer consoles back on Citadel I.

Flash, Dale, and Zarkov stepped up onto the
raised dais and crossed to where Sandra stood
looking down at what apparently was the main
control console, in front of which were a half-
dozen acceleration couches.

When she looked up her eyes were shining. "This
is no different than anything on Citadel I. It *is* a
ship."

Zarkov had brushed past her and was studying
the control board. After a moment he reached out
and punched a series of buttons. The huge dome
overhead darkened, the effect dramatic.

The dais was bathed in a dim red glow as Zarkov
slipped into one of the acceleration couches, which
automatically powered forward, and then leaned
back. The section of control console in front of him
rose into place at his fingertips, the controls themselves lighting up like a Christmas holograph.

He punched another series of buttons, and the
stars appeared in the overhead dome, causing Dale
to gasp. Even Flash could feel his heart quickening.
The effect made it seem as if they had suddenly
been transported outside, the vast bowl of the sky
stretching from horizon to horizon overhead. The

entire dome was a viewscreen-scanner.

Zarkov's fingers were racing over the board as Flash slipped into the center acceleration couch, which powered into position, a wide section of the control console sliding into place at his fingertips. From where he sat he could see and operate the controls and still have an unobstructed view of the dome overhead.

He was in the pilot's position, the controls in front of him no different than the controls aboard the Citadel I shuttle that he had flown. This indeed was a ship.

"I have weapons control," Sandra's voice came to him, seemingly a few centimeters overhead, and he looked over to where she was locked into position in an acceleration couch next to Zarkov's. Beyond her, Dale's acceleration couch was sliding into position, and a section of the control console was rising into place.

"I've got astrogation and scanning," Zarkov said softly, and he turned to look at Flash. "You have the controls?"

"Yes," Flash replied. "How about you, Dale?"

"I'm not sure . . .," she started to say, but she stopped in midsentence. "No, wait . . . I've got life supports, it looks like, and defensive shield, and something else. Maybe communications."

Overhead, the patterns of stars were rapidly shifting as Zarkov did something with the scanning controls, but then the image solidified on a section of space in which tens of thousands of red specks swarmed in formation.

"I'm locking astrogation on the Citadel II ships," he said. "See if you can get us out of here,

Flash, before they begin making the jump. I'd rather take the fight out to them than have it brought here to Centrus."

It seemed impossible that a ship this size could ever fly, just as it seemed impossible that any piece of machinery could work after lying dormant for twenty thousand years. But when Flash reached out and touched the sequencing controls for sub-orbital flight, he could feel instantly the vast ship coming to life.

Sirens sounded throughout the vessel, and as Flash waited for the system's integrity indicators to come green, he half-turned his head. "Dale, how about life supports?"

"All green," Dale's voice came to him from directly overhead.

"Weapons control on and armed," Sandra said, a tinge of excitement in her voice.

All levels on Flash's console went green, and a data screen lit up showing Zarkov's astrogation program, with the ship's yaw, pitch, and roll bubble directly centered.

Flash cranked up the power and hit the manual sequencing control. They began to move. Somehow this vessel, which was more than fifty kilometers in diameter and whose mass Flash guessed was in the trillions of tons, eased itself off the desert floor and accelerated ponderously.

"Switching to optical overlay," Zarkov called out, and the dome overhead suddenly showed the pale blue sky and the planet's horizon around them slipping away as they continued to climb.

Flash alternated his gaze from the primary engine gauges to the altitude indicator and the stabilizers, which were tied in with astrogation.

Everything was going smoothly as the ship continued to accelerate, and he was able to forget the size of the thing he was piloting, because it handled no differently than the Citadel I shuttle craft.

It took them a full three minutes to achieve orbital altitude, and Zarkov once again brought up the scanner display on the dome.

"Intercept hyperpoint plotted," the aging scientist called out.

"Weapons control charged and standing by," Sandra said evenly.

"Defensive shields up and deepening," Dale said with a slight quaver in her voice.

Flash reached out to touch the hyperdrive engine controls but held off a moment as he gazed overhead at the thousands of red dots, each indicating a Citadel II warship.

"The war continues," he mumbled half to himself, and he hit the controls. An instant later the mammoth vessel shot out of real space with a nauseating lurch, and the dome was splashed with a deep blue that shimmered and shifted with swirls of red and violet and green and every color in the spectrum.

"Counting," Zarkov said, and Flash's gaze shifted to his astrogation model, which depicted the ship as a red cross moving slowly toward a three-dimensional target.

Slowly, but inexorably, the cross moved across the screen, until several seconds later it matched the computed course destination. Then the ship came automatically out of hyperdrive back into real space.

In every direction, for as far as the dome could indicate on optical, were Citadel II warships, and the moment the images solidified, control of the huge vessel was automatically taken away from Flash.

As if in some ancient and terrible ballet, the *Ultimus* skipped and danced in and out of hyperspace, moving apparently at random here and there throughout the vast Citadel II warship formation.

Each time the huge vessel came into real space its massive weaponry fired, and hundreds of Citadel II ships winked out of existence, as if they had never been.

Someone was screaming, sirens wailed, the ship's power generators howled, and their defensive screens glowed a brilliant white that made it nearly impossible to look at the dome, but still the destruction continued. In and out of hyperspace they went, and each time the shift came, Flash's stomach flopped over. The battle went on and on, lights racing across their control panels far faster than any human eye could possibly hope to follow.

And suddenly it was over as quickly and as automatically as it had begun, leaving them alone in space. Not even a small piece of wreckage indicated that a vast battle had just taken place.

For several long minutes Flash was too stunned to move, or even to think, as he stared dully up at the dome, which now showed only the stars.

The destruction of the Citadel II forces had been complete, he was certain of it. There was nothing in the galaxy that could resist or defend against the terrible force of this vessel.

Finally he turned in his seat to look over at Zarkov, who stared white-faced up at the dome far overhead.

"Hans," he said, and Zarkov turned his head slowly to look at Flash, but he said nothing.

"We did it," Sandra whooped from where she was seated. "We did it!"

"Hans," Flash said again. "Plot us a course for Citadel I. Let's go back."

Sandra had powered her acceleration couch back, and she climbed out of it and came across to Zarkov's position. He turned away from Flash to look at her.

"They were only machines," she said. "Warships operated by droids. Citadel II will build another fleet. And another, and another."

"The war isn't over?" Zarkov asked in a hoarse voice, and Flash's heart went out to his old friend. Destruction, for whatever reason, was totally alien to the old man.

"No," Sandra said gently. "Not until Citadel II is destroyed. This was only the first battle. Citadel II will not quit. Their machine will analyze this battle, and sooner or later, if we give them the time, they will find a way to counteract this force. This ship is the ultimate weapon only so long as no other force in the galaxy has anything to defeat it with. Just like the crossbow at one time was the ultimate weapon. Just like thermonuclear devices were the ultimate weapon. Just like your laser lances were the ultimate weapon. Ultimate only until someone or something builds an even more powerful device."

For a long time Zarkov just stared at the young

woman, and then without a word he turned back to his astrogation console. Within a couple of minutes he had plotted a return course for Citadel I.

Before he punched the astrogation transfer, which would run the course up on Flash's control console, he once again turned to look at Sandra. "When this is done this machine will be destroyed."

She started to protest, but he cut her off.

"If it means a head-to-head confrontation with you, with Martin, or the computer, I'll do it, Miss Debonshire, make no mistake about it. If it means the destruction of Citadel I, I will still do it. Make no mistake about it."

He reached out and hit the transfer control, and a moment later Flash locked in on the course. The gigantic ship winked into hyperspace with a lurch, and the dome went blank.

They would have a week to figure out exactly what they were going to have to do, Flash thought as he powered his seat back and climbed out of it. It would take that long for their return.

At this point he could understand both Zarkov's and Sandra's feelings. The Citadel II would have to be destroyed. The war would have to be ended once and for all. There was no question about it. And yet this machine could not be allowed to exist any longer than it was needed. Its power would be too great a temptation for man or machine.

Dale had gotten out of her acceleration couch, and she joined them as Flash helped Zarkov down.

"I made a promise to you, Hans," Flash said, and Zarkov looked up at him. "I'll keep it."

The old man nodded, seemingly satisfied, and

for just a brief instant Flash could see battles yet to be fought, destruction beyond anything they had yet seen, and problems confronting them, that at the moment none of them could comprehend. And for that same brief instant Flash wished with everything in his soul that none of this had ever happened, that they could all be back on Earth.

It was a war of the Citadels, he thought. Computer against computer. Machine against machine. A war in which man had no business. He only hoped that somehow they all would survive it, because it was a war that none of them could turn their backs on any longer.